Chase & Kassidy

All Eyes On Us

By

MyKisha Mac

&

Tysha Jordyn

FR.

Remember....
You haven't read 'til you've read #Royalty
Check us out at www.royaltypublishinghouse.com
#royaltydropsdopebooks

Text ROYALTY to 42828 for sneak peeks and
notifications when they come out!

Looking for a publishing home?

Royalty Publishing House, Where the Royals reside, is accepting submissions for writers in the urban fiction genre. If you're interested, submit the first 3-4 chapters with your synopsis to submissions@royaltypublishinghouse.com. Check out our website for more information: www.royaltypublishinghouse.com.

CPSIA information can be obtained
at www.ICGtesting.com
Printed in the USA
LVHW04s2302180518
577693LV00011B/719/P

9 781519 110237

Be sure to <u>LIKE</u> our Royalty Publishing House
page on Facebook

Other Novels Written By MyKisha Mac:

The Love of a Good Man
Introducing Star IV
Hate That I Love You 1 & 2
Sky & Sincere: His Rider, Her Roller
1 & 2

~

Coming Soon:
Sky & Sincere: His Rider, Her Roller
3

Other Novels Written By Tysha Jordyn:

I Should've Cheated (*pen name TJ Rose*)

Love, Betrayal, & Dirty Money: A Hood Romance (*anthology; pen name TJ Rose*)

Love The Way You Thug Me

~

Coming Soon

Love The Way You Thug Me 2 (Dec 2015)

I Should've Cheated Too (Dec 2015)

Money, Power, and Sins: The Cartwright Family (Dec 2015)

Love, Betrayal, & Dirty Money 2 (Late 2015/Early 2016)

Prologue

"Mmmm, I got sumthin' to fill ya mouth, gurl," Chase smiled.

"You promise, cause all I'm hearin' is talk....we'll see what you workin' with when you touch down. When are you coming back anyway, babe?" Kassidy cooed.

"Soon ma," Chase began, but paused as he turned onto the unpaved trail leading up to the safe house. "Ay ma, lemme hit you back in a lil' bit," Chase hesitated.

Ending the call, Chase stopped his truck a few feet short of the fence that hugged the property line, just beyond the eyeshot of the house. Sliding out of the driver seat, he softly eased the door shut, then took long, deliberate steps toward the house, tiptoeing across the gravel. *Something's off, shit ain't right,* he thought to himself as his feet came to rest at the trunk base of a Dominican Magnolia tree, which was in full bloom. Stilling his respirations, he slipped into his zone, shutting out all stimuli and clearing his head to assess just what the fuck had caused the eerie silence.

Drawing a deep breath in through his nostrils, Chase's sinuses were greeted by a pungent odor that he was all too familiar with-fresh gunpowder. *Fuck,* he silently cursed, a sense of alarm settling deep in his gut as he dreaded the scene that likely awaited him inside. *Perfect hideout in plain sight my ass.* Retrieving his phone from his pocket, he pressed his right thumbprint onto the home button, unlocking the device. Swiping right twice, he opened the iCam app and disabled the cameras that surveilled the home's exterior before returning the phone to his pocket.

Crossing the yard and hugging the right exterior wall of the home, Chase crept just under the first window, coming to rest underneath the second and only window that would afford him a 360 view of most of the first floor. Retrieving a small square of plastic from his pocket, he flipped it over, extended it a few inches from his

face, and angled the mirrored back to face the window. Rotating the mirror from left to right a few times, he took in the view. *No bodies...the fuck is them niggas at?*

Chase side-stepped the remainder of the wall and arrived at the back door. Glock 40 drawn, he glanced around the backyard, hurdled the trip wire, and quickly ascended the stairs to step onto the oak floor just beyond the threshold. Body hugging the staircase, Chase eased toward the front entry of the home, pausing as he cleared one room after another. As he approached the third room to his left, he froze mid-step when he heard a faint rustling. Just as he craned his neck to hone in on the sound, the door came crashing open.

BLAH! BLAH! BLAH!

Chase dove away from the door just as a round zipped past his left temple; his right shoulder met the rigid floor with a thud as he returned fire, both set of rounds now mixed in a drafty joust.

"Ahh fuck!" Chase hissed as a bullet ricocheted off the doorframe and pierced his left forearm. He slid across the floor, briefly retreating into the alcove provided by the previous doorway. Just as his back came to rest on the door, he heard a flurry of footsteps approach him. Wasting no time, he leaned forward, took aim outside the doorway, and started to empty his clip.

"Shit! Get back! Get back!" He heard the voice of a man throw a panicked warning to someone else, but it was too late. Chase looked on as the bodies of both men hit the floor–one face up, eyes glazed over in distress, and the other stretched out on his stomach, a mess of curls obscuring his forehead.

"Ugh...fuck...ahh..." curly top groaned, a stream of blood flowing onto the floor from his mouth.

Chase replaced his spent clip, briefly applied pressure to his wound, then rose to his feet and took a few short steps, stopping just short of the curly top's head.

"Turn over, nigga," Chase ordered, nudging the man's shoulder with his foot.

"Fuck you!" the man spat in return; Chase chuckled as he locked eyes with him, sending a sharp kick to the man's stomach; now doubled over in pain, the man obliged Chase's request.

"Coño!" the man moaned.

"You joining ya homie ova there? Or you gon' tell me how the fuck you found my spot?" Chase quizzed.

"Maldito hijo de la porra, veta pa la porra!" curly top willed Chase to take a trip to hell.

"You first," Chase smiled just before he sent two rounds into the man, one to the dome, one to the chest.

Chapter 1

Nine Months Earlier

"Mmm…shit…love…this…dick."

Chase rammed all ten inches of his manhood as deep as he could, trying to tickle her ovaries with the tip. Slowing his stroke for a brief second, he smiled down at his *Friday* chick.

Bitch think she slick talkin' bout love and shit, he thought to himself. Tomeka was a cool ass chick he met in Atlantic City last summer. He was leaving his boy Lando's bachelor party at the Borgata, and ran into her on the boardwalk. Her 38 DDs were peeking out her crop top, just begging to be tongue lashed, and the mix of 'dro and Henny had Chase all too happy to oblige. Tomeka just knew she had that fire pussy, and swore she was gonna ride him all the way into a happily ever after, but that was the last thing on Chase's mind. *I don't wife them, I one-night them,* was Chase's motto, and he relished every second of his stick and move lifestyle.

"Yesssss daddy…this Meka's dick…shit…all Meka's dick," she subconsciously claimed her stake in Chase, throwing her ass back in a circle and making it bounce back against Chase's firm six-pack.

"Damn ma, this shit so…fuckin…wet," Chase moaned, feeling his climax approaching. As much as he wanted to lay in her shit all night, he had moves to make–plus, the longer he laid and played with Tomeka, the more she had them wifey ambitions.

"Ooooooooo Chase…I'm bout ta…mmm…bout ta cummm," she cooed, her breathing ragged in anticipation of her explosive orgasm.

"Shit, let it go ma," Chase coaxed as he succumbed to his own explosion. "Fuuuuuuck ma, shiiiiit, damn this some good pussy…SHIIIIIT!"

"Damn I love you nigga, I love you...FUCK, I love you!" Tomeka screamed.

Yeah, it's bout time to switch up my rotation, this chick is all outta pocket, Chase thought to himself as he emptied the last of his seeds into the Magnum. Satisfied that Tomeka would be out for the night, Chase slid off the edge of the bed and headed to the bathroom to hop in the shower. He was meeting up with his crew at Club Ménage in a little bit to chop it up about business.

"Bae, where you going? Come lay with me," Tomeka whined.

"Ay, what I tell you 'bout callin' me that? And I got moves to make ma, so I'm 'bout to bounce."

"Damn, you always on that hit and run shit," she pouted.

"Look baby girl, you know what it is, so I don't even know why you acting like we all boo'd up and shit, fuck outta here with all that," Chase quipped, making his way to the shower.

Reaching into the shower, he turned the dial and adjusted the water temperature to his preference. As he waited for the water stream to heat up all the way, he gave himself a once over in the mirror. Readjusting the elastic band that held his locks into place, he brushed his hand along his jawline and smiled to himself. Standing at 6'4, Chase had a deep, dark chocolate complexion, courtesy of his Haitian roots. He was a health nut and was fiercely picky about what entered his temple, so he was faithful to his daily workout regimen; his chiseled, rock-hard physique was evidence of his fitness addiction.

Steam now consuming the wall-to-wall mirror, Chase stripped out of his wife beater and socks and stepped into the scalding stream of water. Pressing his hands into the wall of the shower, he leaned forward, allowing the custom settings of Tomeka's showerhead to massage his shoulders; he groaned, enjoying varied water pressure as his mind drifted far away from Tomeka. He tried to focus on the serious lick he was about to hit, and the next moves his crew was going to make, but he couldn't

escape the boredom he always felt the minute he finished smashing one of his jump offs. Chase had never been a one-woman man, but no amount of pussy ever seemed to be enough. He'd smashed all shapes and shades of chicks, and he had yet to run up one that fully satisfied him.

Tomeka's knock at the bathroom door interrupted his thoughts, so he knew he had to raise up out of her spot quick, before she started that *let's cuddle* shit again. He quickly lathered the shower pouf Tomeka kept for him, scrubbed and rinsed away the Friday sex from his flesh, and climbed out.

"Why you lock the door baby? I was gon' join you," Tomeka whined.

"I'm good on that ma," Chase scoffed, biting his tongue so he wouldn't curse her ass out. Satisfied his locks were towel-dried enough, he snatched the door open, slid back into his clothes, and grabbed his keys.

"You comin' back later? I'm not done," Tomeka asked.

"But I am," Chase called over his shoulder as he headed downstairs, yanked the front door open, and slammed it behind him.

Just as Chase pulled out of Tomeka's condo complex, his phone vibrated in his lap.

"Speak," Chase answered.

"Ay my nigga, shit's thick up in the spot tonight, where you at, yo?"

"Nigga you the boss now?" Chase joked with Lando, his right hand.

"Bruh you know what it is," Lando laughed. "But ay, we off in the cut, get at me, nigga."

"Aight, bet," Chase ended the call.

He made the drive from Tomeka's spot out in Heartland Village to Club Ménage in silence as he let his thoughts keep him company. He toyed with the idea of sliding back through Tomeka's spot later on for another round, but decided against it since he knew

she'd be all touchy feely and shit. *Fuck I look like playin' house and shit,* he mused to himself.

Twenty minutes later, Chase was easing his Yukon Denali into the valet lane at the club. Met at the curb by a female attendant, Chase flashed his panty-droppimg smile, tossed her the keys to his ride, and winked at her as he headed into the club. *Bet her panties wet already,* he smiled to himself at how the attendant had just eye-fucked him.

That nigga Lando wasn't lyin', it's thick as a muthafucka up in this bitch tonight, Chase observed. Scanning the room real quick, he was able to take in the whole scene from where he stood; the first floor was packed body to body with all the young heads, and the second tier was buzzing with the 25 and up cats dressed to the nines. As usual, there was a line trailing from the third tier, which was VIP, as chicks sucked in guts, poked out asses, and pushed titties up, hoping to catch the eye of just the right baller and be granted a spot for the night. Chase spotted his crew in their usual booth up top and slid through the crowd to head up that way.

"Damn daddi, I'm goin' wit you?" some young ass chick that looked barely legal, flirted as she reached for Chase's arm. Shaking his head, he continued on until he made it up the stairs and past the velvet rope that kept the have nots from mingling with the haves.

Chapter 2

"Damn girl, you ain't ready yet?" Mia prodded her friend, Kassidy.

"Bih, why you in such a rush? Damn, ain't like you got a man you meeting and shit," Kassidy eyed her friend in the vanity mirror, rolling her eyes as she continued giving the last few strands of her mane a bone-straight press with her flat iron.

"And ain't gon' come up on one either with how slow ya ass movin', trick," Mia popped her lips as she gave the mirror her side profile, making sure her dress pimped out her wide hips and ample ass just right.

"Remind me again why the hell we just *gooooootttta* step out tonight? Shit, *Empire* comes on tonight," Kassidy sighed, slightly irritated that her friend was yet again dragging her out to a club. The saying opposites attract rang quite true in Kassidy and Mia's case; Kassidy was an introverted homebody who was content to curl up with a good book, sip some tea, and blow some trees. Mia, on the other hand, was the queen of the turn up, and was guaranteed to make an appearance at all the hottest parties and clubs.

Kassidy Kingston was the daughter of Maria and Kameron Kingston. While Maria was the true definition of a stay-at-home wife, Kameron was addicted to the thrill of the streets—on the legit side. A longtime officer with the US Marshals, he had been promoted to his current post as Special Agent in Charge of the High Intensity Drug Trafficking Area (HIDTA) task force about a year ago. Though he was accustomed to getting his hands dirty on the daily, investigating dealers and connects, Kameron took pride in the one thing in his life that was pristine and chaste—his precious Kassidy. He took pride in being able to provide Kassidy, her two younger siblings, and her mom with a sheltered life in the Southeast Annadale area of Staten Island, far away from the grimy streets of the borough.

Kameron spared no expense shielding his oldest daughter away from the fast cars, dope boys, and street thugs who he investigated and brought to justice daily. He had other plans for his baby girl KK, as he affectionately called her. Ensuring that she graduated from the prestigious Staten Island Academy, Kameron had dreams of Kassidy going on to study psychology, possibly joining the Behavioral Science Unit with the FBI. He figured that if he drowned Kassidy with all the perks and benefits of working on the right side of the law, there was no way she'd ever fall victim to the temptation of loving a thug–made perfect sense in his mind. Kameron drilled *'bad boys brings babies'* into Kassidy's head so deep that she never even thought about talking to one, let alone dating one; she was a good girl, daddy's pride and joy, and had big dreams of becoming everything her father wanted her to become.

"Bih, you *goooooottttta* step out tonight cuz' you need to get them cobwebs knocked out ya cooch, and that ain't gon' happen with you all hugged up wit da damn TV!"

"But why come? Jussie Smollett is gonna miss me if I ain't rockin' with him tonight," Kassidy whined.

"DVR his ass because he wants the same thing you want anyway. That's one dick you won't be riding. Now come on chick!" Mia pressed.

"I'm comin' damn, always hot in the ass to slide up in VIP somewhere," Kassidy huffed at Mia's impatience, wondering just which nigga's face Mia would be all up in that night.

Mia Maddison, Kassidy's best friend, was her polar opposite. Growing up far away from the posh suburban American dream that Kassidy was accustomed to, Mia had other plans for her life after high school, none of which included her working hard at anything except throwing her ass. Mia pursued ballers like she pursued a wet dream; all she saw was fast cars, money, and the baller who could give it to her. She'd watched her mother and stepfather struggle to make ends meet growing up, and knew at a young age that living paycheck to paycheck was not the business.

Mia was one of those girls who only hooked up with dudes whose names were ringing in the streets. If his status wasn't baller, Mia wasn't checking for him and would never give him the time of day. Chase knew she was the typical chick who only saw dollar signs, and was willing to do just about anything to get a piece of the riches, which is why he'd been sure to curve her thirsty attempts in the past.

Mia was a deliciously caramel mixture of Dominican and Haitian heritage. Although her Dominican genes dominated her Haitian genes and were nearly undetectable, Mia used all her physical assets to her advantage. Standing at 5'9 with legs for days, Mia's ample bosom, hips, thighs, and ass always turned heads, and she knew just how to flaunt it. Truth be told, it was her that caught the eye of most guys in the room when they stepped out, not Kassidy. Unfortunately, she had a knack for turning even the thirstiest nigga off the minute she opened her mouth.

"Alright damn, we rollin' now?" Kassidy sighed as she pranced down the hallway toward her living room, stopping to check herself out in the full-length mirror just outside of her foyer.

"Yasss, now let's go!" Mia rushed as they both slipped into their Valentinos, grabbed their purses and phones, and headed out the door. Kassidy paused on her front porch momentarily, using the fob on her keyring to arm her security system. Seeing Mia stomping off toward her own ride, Kassidy gave pause.

"Uh, I ain't hardly about to let you drive when I know your ass is gonna be gone by the end of the night off them shots, I'LL be the designated driver," Kassidy stressed.

"Girl, ain't nobody gonna get drunk! Shit, Imma just get me a lil buzz and chill, why you so damn square? I'll drive," Mia countered.

"Nah girl, I'm good on that, I'll drive; plus, you know I can't drive a damn stick, so I'm not tryin' to be stuck calling a cab when your ass decides to creep off with some nigga," Kassidy laughed.

"Fine, shit, you gonna make sure I wear my seatbelt too, *mommy*?" Mia teased.

"Damn right, somebody need to strap your wild ass down somewhere, at least all the husbands in town would be safe for the night," Kassidy laughed at her own joke.

"Ay, if the home is happy, then ya man won't be passing out the dick like it's trick or treat season," Mia affirmed her hoe stroll philosophy.

"Whatever chick, come on before my time limit in these pumps expires," Kassidy laughed as the two friends slid into Kassidy's Audi S5 and headed to Club Ménage.

Chapter 3

After a long day of salon and spa treatments, fucking up some commas in the mall, slaying hair, and beating faces, they arrived at the club. The valet parked Kassidy's ride while they did their last minute checks before walking in the club. Security stamped their hands, and they entered the club as Mia threw a flirtatious wink at the Ving Rhames lookalike that worked the door.

Their eyes scanned the crowd and building for a few moments, taking in the vibe. Just as they were about to head to the bar, the DJ lured their ears with "679" by Fetty Wap. Mia made a beeline for the dance floor as she began to move her hips with the tempo of the beat. She swirled her voluptuous hips side to side, as if she was a belly dancer from Egypt putting on a show for an Egyptian King, hoping that he would choose her for the night. Slightly raising one hand up and gliding her other hand down her leg and ass, Mia stole the attention of several thirsty eyes for a brief moment. Neon blinking lights circled the room as other club hoppers took the dance floor and cut a rug. All the while, Kassidy hung back at the bar, slightly swaying her hips to the music although her mind was elsewhere.

Yasss...that's my shit right there, Mia thought to herself as she raised her hand, then lifted her long hair up with her arms. Mia seduced the room with her seductive moves, turning her attention to the third tier, which housed the VIP sections. To her delight, her gaze landed on a top-notch specimen, and she worked overtime eyeballing the most eligible hitta in the building–the rich chocolate, high roller by the name of Chase Baptiste. No doubt the subject of many wet dreams all up and through the borough, Mia was well aware that Chase's Holy Trinity consisted of three things: money, pussy, and taking over the world. By her blueprint, she'd provide the pussy, which would motivate Chase to provide her with the money, and together they'd both take over the world–a girl can dream, right?

Two songs later, Mia and Kassidy needed a break and a drink. Mia pointed to an empty table as she led Kassidy to the spot that they would occupy. Thankfully, the waitress met them just as they slid into their seats, and took their order for a round of bottle service.

"Girl, it's a full house tonight. I better snatch me a baller before the night is over," Mia jested.

Kassidy sat with her legs crossed and flipped her long bangs out of her face. She gazed around the room and watched the dancers as they owned the floor.

"I don't know Mia…maybe I should have stayed home tonight. I'm just not feeling it. I could be watching my show rather than wasting time," Kassidy exhaled, her mood apparent by the unbothered scowl on her face.

"Anywhere sexy ass Chase is at could never be a waste of my time. Mmm hmm…nigga know he fine as fuck. What a bitch won't do to get a taste of that chocolate stick," Mia said as she bit her bottom lip, thinking about all the little naughty things she would like to do to him.

"Chase? Who's he?"

"Bitch, Chase Baptiste. You don't know him?"

"Nah, never heard of him. Should I know him?"

"Girl?! I'm shocked you don't and YES…he is definitely a nigga you should know. And if you don't know him, by all means you should get to know him. That nigga is one hundred percent certified General status."

"He ain't no Barack Obama, so nah, I'm good," Kassidy said playfully as she turned her nose up.

Mia looked over at Chase again, giving him puppy dog eyes and trying to catch his attention, but she noticed his attention seemed to be elsewhere. She looked at Kassidy, who was in her own little world, and then looked back at Chase. *One of us got to leave with his number tonight. If not me, then why not my girl? Shit, maybe I can slide up next to Lando's sexy ass instead–close enough, right?*

"Yeah okay, but I bet that nigga feelin' you."

"What are you talking about, Mia? Ain't nobody got time for your matchmaker, love connection ish. I'm tellin' you right now, I'm not interested. I got other shit on my mind right now. You know my daddy on my ass about school, and that nigga is working my last damn nerve. I don't need any more distractions."

"Girl, screw your daddy-and I do mean I'd fuck his fine ass...with his Michael Ealy lookin' ass. I thought you were takin' some time though, so what's the rush? Girl, you betta live your damn life, you ain't no lil kid no more. You know I haven't said two words to my parents since I found out that they been hiding shit from me. I mean...who does that? My parents are something else for sure, but Kameron Kingston? Nah, he's a whole 'nother level."

"Girl tell me about it, but you know that man is not gonna let up on me for nothing," Kassidy sighed and continued to look at Mia. "Mannn yeah...that was really fucked up what your parents kept from you though. How could they keep something so important from you? I'm still trying to figure that shit out for real. And as for as Kam Kingston...I'm in my own shit and he's still riding me about school, like I'm not gonna ever go back. It ain't that I don't wanna finish, but...I don't know. Shit, maybe I just shoulda stayed in and finished; at least by now I'd be done with grad school and headed to medical school."

"Girl bye–you did what you felt you needed to do, but enough with all this parents/ school talk, and being responsible and focused shit. We ain't come here to talk about yo' pops–unless you gonna hook me up–"

"Really Mia!" Kassidy interrupted.

"What? I'm just sayin'...but for real, just chill with all that stressing shit. Ain't like you no dummy; you smart, so you'll figure it all out but in the meantime…that nigga Chase can't keep his eyes off you–look. Let's go over there and holla at him!"

"Umm…I don't think so. Didn't I tell you I didn't want to get hooked up tonight?" Kassidy replied as her eyes drifted across

the VIP section and landed on Chase. He looked to be deep in conversation with his boys, and as much as Kassidy said she didn't want to be hooked up, she couldn't pull herself from his pearly white smile, deep almond eyes, and oh so suckable lips. *Damn*, she thought to herself as she felt a slight tingle beneath the lacy La Perlas that cloaked her goodies.

"Well if not that, let's dance some more then," Mia jested as she got up from her seat and grabbed Kassidy by the hand, and persuading her on to the dance floor.

Mia and Kassidy danced to the sound of *All Eyes on Us* by Meek Mill and Nicki Minaj. Mia playfully sang along with Nicki's part.

Now it's all eyes on us, and this all lies on trust
And if them bitches wanna trip, tell 'em they tour guides on
us

The night was young and full of possibilities; Kassidy hoped she could push her school worries far enough to the back of her mind to enjoy the night out, while Mia hoped to run up on a hitta to stretch her legs to the moon later on.

Chapter 4

"Ay niggas, what's good?" Chase side-hugged and dapped each of his boys before he sat down.

"Damn nigga, you climbed out the pussy and shit?" Lando joked.

"Nigga, how 'bout you just worry 'bout makin' sure yo' wife don't light that ass up tonight–ain't you out past curfew and shit?"

"Fuck you nigga, she don't run shit," Lando replied.

"Aight nigga, whateva, what that weather lookin' like tho?" Chase quizzed, talking in their usual code since he didn't want the thots hugged up on his crew all in their business.

"Man, sky's clear, sun's shining, life's good," Lando replied, relaying that all their drops went well, and that each spot paid up with no shorts.

"That's what's up, I dig it," Chase concurred, distracted for a second by the hazel-eyed chick that was frowning a few booths down in another section of VIP. Ms. Hazel Eyes looked real uncomfortable, like she had other shit to do, and when Chase's eyes came to rest on her booth mate, he instantly understood why. *The fuck a fly ass chick like that doin' runnin' with Mia's bird ass?*

Mia was a true jump-off, but not your average jump-off; she had her own shit, but she had some deep ass trap queen dreams, so any good sense she had was lost in her cloud of hood ambitions. She was one of those chicks that tried too damn hard to be up close and personal with the hood life. Determined to fuck her way to the top, she'd tried more than a few times to slide up next to Chase, but he didn't even blink at her ass. She stayed on come-up mode 24/7, and all the fellas knew she had no brand loyalty; whichever baller was popping at the moment, that's whose dick she'd ride. Mia had tried to get at Chase before, but he shut her down because game recognized game. Although Mia was pleasing to eyes, there was something about her that didn't sit well with Chase–aside from her

thottish ways. He couldn't put his finger on it, but her in-crowd mentality didn't intrigue him one way or another.

Blocking Mia out like she wasn't even there, Chase kept stealing glances at the butter pecan cutie. Her innocent loveliness enticed his manhood as he couldn't take his eyes off her. Chase could tell she wasn't the average around the way girl, and there was something hypnotic about her look that trapped his eyes. Taking a sip of his Hennessey, Chase slipped into a casual conversation with Lando and the rest of his crew, still watching Ms. Butta Pecan from the corner of his eye. Smiling as he got lost in his thoughts for a moment, he licked his lips in anticipation of making her his girl for the night.

***

With the grand opening of his new sports bar in full swing, Lando was all smiles and high off the success of his new business venture. All the nights of being cursed out by his wife seemed worth it in that moment. Being Chase's right hand kept him in the streets and away from home long enough, but getting Premier Lounge up and running had him and his wife basically passing one another like ships in the night. The more he thought to himself, Lando realized he had to take the blame for much of that. Where most newlyweds were still tired from fucking like rabbits, the flame between him and his wife had fizzled shortly after they said their *I do's*. Lando knew that deep down he was avoiding dealing with the issue of his failed marriage, but that was an issue for another time and place; tonight night was all about his success, and whatever chick he might choose to entertain him for the night.

Chase observed Kassidy and Mia twirling around the floor. There were plenty of tens floating around the club, but Chase only had eyes for one. To his own surprise, he wasn't checking out other women; he was more interested in knowing who Kassidy was. Chase was always up in Ménage, but this was the first time he'd seen Kassidy there. Kassidy finally noticed Chase eyeing her as she swayed her hips and treaded the floor. She glanced back and gave

him a subtle smile, and that was all the ammunition he needed to know that she might be interested. Chase continued to sip his drink and feign interest in the conversation with his boys, as he undressed Kassidy with his eyes, paying particular attention to what seemed like a set of endless legs. *Mmm, them legs up on my shoulders,* he smiled to himself.

"Yo nigga...if you watch that bitch any harder, she might think you stalking her stuck up ass," Lando joked.

"Nigga what you talking 'bout? I ain't gotta stalk no bitch, you already know I gets mine. I just like what I see. So you think she stuck up?"

"You don't? Look at her pretty ass, she looking like Kerry Washington, all prissy and shit, she ain't hardly 'bout to get down with no hood as nigga like you."

"Whateva bruh, but ay, Imma catch y'all niggas later. I got some shit I need to hit. Get at me later," Chase said as he stood up and dapped Lando off with another side hug.

"Aight nigga, be easy. I'll hit you later if the weather changes."

"That's wassup," Chase said as he gave Lando and the rest of the clique a military salute and headed out of VIP.

Chase headed down the stairs and walked through the dance floor, headed toward the exit. As he tried to make his way through the crowd, the same young chick who snatched at his arm when he first got there pulled at the bottom of his shirt. Chase turned his head when he felt the youngster pulling at him.

"I guess you didn't hear me the first time. Daddi, can I roll with you?"

Without hesitation Chase smiled, "Nah baby girl, I ain't that nigga. Hit me up in a couple of years though and I may think about it." *The fuck wrong with you, nigga ain't trying to catch a case,* he thought.

Chase continued to walk through the maze of the dance floor, which was packed with people shoulder to shoulder, and ass to ass.

He brushed up against Kassidy's back, the bulge in his pants purposely grazing her ass. *The fuck*, Kassidy thought as she turned her head to the side to see what nigga was trying to dry hump all up on her. Out of the corner of her eye, she noticed it was the same cat Mia was going on and on about up in VIP, the same one that ignited the tingle down below for her earlier, the cat with the dreadlocks who she'd just caught watching her like a hawk in VIP–Mr. Chase Baptiste.

With a subtle smile, Kassidy slowly turned her head back, facing the crowd as she pretended not to notice that Chase's dick was poking her. *I know damn well he knows his dick is on my ass. This nigga is some kind of bold but uh uh uhn...he surely got me curious*, Kassidy thought to herself.

Chase confidently placed his hand on Kassidy's side as he slowly slid by her and made sure she felt every inch of him up against her backside. *You fucking tease*, Kassidy continued to think to herself as her nipples hardened and her pussy thumped. Chase continued to walk, trying to exit the club just as Mia noticed him leaving. *Damn, lemme get at his fine ass real quick*, Mia thought to herself. Thirsty as always, she wasn't about to let Chase slide up out the club without trying to put at least one of them on with his fine ass. Mia tapped him on the shoulder, and Chase turned around with a wicked stare. Kassidy just stood back watching, but was secretly glad Mia stopped Chase before he left, because she slyly wanted to get another look at the mouth-watering specimen of a man that he was, whether she was willing to admit it to Mia or not.

Chase gawked at Mia. He didn't despise Mia, but he knew what Mia was all about and he was tired of telling her that he wasn't interested in her trap queen advances. *Oh it's you, what the fuck do you want?*

"What up Chase? Leaving so early?"

"What up ma, yeah I'm 'bout to dip out," Chased answered disengaged, shifting his gaze to Kassidy as he bit his bottom lip and winked at her.

"From the looks of it, I don't think you're ready to leave at all," Mia said as she watched him drool over Kassidy. Chase turned his attention back towards Mia.

"Is that right?"

"Bet. Yo...check this out. I can help you get that if you're really interested."

Chase gave Mia a bizarre stare as he was trying to figure out her angle. He knew Mia was slick with the tongue, and if she was willing to help him, there had to be something in it for her. Mia always had a hidden agenda, and she would stop at nothing to get what she wanted. Mia wanted in, and she was willing to sacrifice Kassidy if that's what it took to get close to Chase.

"You got my attention, now what you gonna do with it? Time is money."

Mia leaned in and whispered in Chase's ear. "Time and place, and I'll make sure she's there."

Chase leaned back for a second, giving Mia a quizzical stare. *The fuck shorty so pressed for me to get at her girl for,* he thought to himself. Fortunate for him, his desire to bed Kassidy had hijacked his thoughts for the moment, so if Mia had an in for him that didn't involve him having to sweet talk Kerry Washington's little sister, he was going to roll with it.

"Aight, tomorrow evening, 6:00 at Wolfe's Pond. Better be worth my while. Like I said...time is money and I don't have time to be fucking around, feel me?" Chase said as he turned around and walked off.

Oh it will definitely be worth your while, playboy. You can believe that, with your sexy ass. Nothing in this world is free, and I know just how you can show your gratitude.

Mia walked back towards Kassidy, who had a low-key jealous look on her face.

"Bitch what? Why you looking at me like that?"

Kassidy shook her head. "You know why, tramp. You hookin' up with him later, huh? I saw you all in his ear and shit."

"No, not at all, but he did invite me to meet up tomorrow night. And he was very clear about bringing you along," Mia smiled.

"Really? Why he didn't just ask me himself then? He was all up on my ass getting a free roll and shit, but he failed to mention that he was having a private party tomorrow night."

"Shit, I don't know if it's a private party or not and maybe because he knew your sadity ass wouldn't take the invitation."

Kassidy laughed.

"Bitch I am not sadity."

"Kass...you are, you just don't see it, but everybody else around you does. If you weren't my girl, I wouldn't even fuck with you like that myself," Mia quipped, suddenly turning her attention to her manicured nails, giving Kassidy a nonchalant brush off with a raised brow. Kassidy continued to laugh.

"Bitch please...if I wasn't your girl, I wouldn't even fuck with *you* like that. You and your hoeish ambitions," Kassidy teased.

"You know what they say, birds of a feather flock together," Mia smiled.

"Well shit, I guess I'm a hoe too according to everybody else," Kassidy frowned as Mia chuckled.

"And what's wrong with being a hoe? I would rather be a hoe than a slut any day," Mia chuckled.

"Really Mia, you gotta be kidding me, right? It's pretty much the same thing. Your ass is crazy," Kassidy laughed.

"No college girl, there's a big difference. You see...a hoe gets paid to lay on her back and a slut just lets these niggas run all up in her for free. She just likes fucking and the attention she gets from them thirsty ass niggas. A hoe be like...*nah nigga put the money on the nightstand before anything even pops off*–that's the difference."

"And that's your philosophy, right?" Kassidy teased.

"Nah, that's the philosophy of the streets. Hey, I didn't make the rules, I just fuck by 'em."

"Well in that case, come on hoe because eyezzz ready to go. My feet are killing me and I can't wait to get some shut eye."

"Yeah I know, so you can dream about Chase and how you wanna taste that homegrown, authentic Haitian protein. Bitch you ain't fooling nobody. You know you wanna saddle up."

"Whatever Mia, not everybody is looking for money left on the nightstand. I told you, I have other shit to think about and it's definitely not Chance, Chase, or whatever his name is."

"Oh bitch, you know his name. You definitely know his name. So are you rollin' tomorrow or what?" Mia laughed.

"How 'bout I just shoot the messenger, because obviously she hasn't heard a word I said tonight."

"Oh I heard you, I'm just not buying it."

Chapter 5

Kassidy and Mia ended a night full of fun with plans of hooking up with Chase the next day. Mia was right; Kassidy seemed unbothered by Chase, but was secretly smitten by his charm. She was typically a good girl with good intentions, but she was flirting with the idea of getting to know the infamous bad boy Chase Baptiste. He was tempting, easy on the eyes, and had the streets on lock from what Mia said. Kassidy figured Chase could have any woman he wanted, and him leaving the club alone that night was probably just by choice. She noticed the way other women tried to flock to Chase like flies flocked to shit; even her girl Mia was trying to get in where she fit in.

Kassidy tried to convince herself that she didn't need any distractions in her life, especially since she had to endure her dad's daily lectures on how she was a college dropout and shamed their family name with her lack of ambition. In spite of her current pool of uncertainty, Kassidy was sure of one thing though-she had to get back on track, and fast. With a daddy like Kameron Kingston, there was no way she was not going to finish college, or end up living paycheck to paycheck.

Kameron had high hopes for Kassidy and if it was totally up to him, she would still have her ass in school and far away from the likes of Mia. Kameron knew there were a lot of distractions in the world, especially thug ass niggas like Chase that wanted to snag a 'good girl' and make her a trophy wife. He saw it every day at work–drug kingpin rules the streets with an iron fist, but has his ride or die trophy wife tucked away somewhere on a pedestal, and when the Feds came knocking, the trophy wife was left with nothing but the designer threads on her back. He didn't want Kassidy getting caught up in that kind of drama.

Kassidy respected her father, but she also had ideas of her own; things that she knew he wouldn't approve of. She often felt like

she was caught in a real-life tug of war as she had Mia in her ear trying to convince her to live her own life and stop letting daddy make decisions for her, while her father was in the other ear preaching about school and a successful career. Kassidy actually agreed with Mia, and she had every intention on showing daddy dearest that she was no longer a little girl, and that she had become a woman.

With the allure of life in the fast lane constantly calling her, Mia felt she hit payload with Chase at the club that night. Getting close to him was only a stepping stone to put her plans in motion. She too, like every other woman in Staten Island, found Chase to be *that nigga*, but Mia saw more. She saw an open door to Chase's inner circle, which would no doubt be an opportunity to hand select the hitta she'd trick into wifing her up. In all the time she'd been trying to slide her way up next to Chase, she'd never seen him as taken with a chick as he was with Kassidy, so she figured convincing Kassidy to hook up with him was a sure way to get her foot in the door.

The next day, Mia and Kassidy met up for their bi-weekly session of hotbox yoga. Kassidy always complained because she hated sweating her hair out and having to re-press her curls to revive her sleek, straight hairstyle. Mia, on the other hand, knew if she wanted to continue to turn heads, she had to keep her figure right and keep it tight. She was curvy, but in all the right places. Everything was perfectly proportioned, so Mia took pride in maintaining her assets. Unlike Mia, Kassidy had a naturally slim build like a supermodel–not the ones who looked like they were missing meals or shoving their fingers down their throats, though. Kassidy was more like Selita Ebanks or Nicole Murphy. She had ass, breasts, honeyed skin, and eyes that would capture any man's attention. Kassidy wasn't a fitness freak, but she did workout just as faithfully as Mia.

"Kass, I don't even know why you gonna sit there and act all unbothered and shit, you know you wanna roll with me to see your

boo tonight," Mia teased, taking her bottled water to the head as they finished up a round of hot box yoga at the gym.

"Here you go with that mess again-I do *not* have a boo Mia, and if you're talking about your lil crush from the club last night, it seems like you're more pressed to get up with him than I am," Kassidy clapped back, wiping the sweat from her brow.

"Look, all I'm sayin' is obviously he's interested if he invited us out, right? You know how paid that nigga is? Shit, what fool is gonna pass up on a chance to be all up and through his space?" Mia bantered.

"Where y'all goin' anyway?"

"*WE,* as in *YOU AND ME* are gonna meet up with him at Wolfe's Pond–"

"Hold up, a damn park? The hell y'all plan on doing, playin' football or something? Wait, I know exactly what y'all plan on doing, with your nasty ass...Mia, you better not smash that man in no damn public park," Kassidy scolded.

"And if I did? Girl you too damn uptight, that's what ya problem is, you need a real nigga like Chase to stretch that thang out!"

"Shut up! You are so damn common, Mia, I swear–you have no damn chill!"

"And you love me for it. Now come on and let's go, we gotta meet his panty wettin' ass in a few hours," Mia prodded, grabbing her friend's hands and pulling her up from her yoga mat.

"I swear, the things I do for your ass..." Kassidy whined, slightly irritated that Mia was so damn anxious to be up in Chase's face. Oh, she had every intention of going–she wouldn't dare miss a personal invite from the sexy dread head, but she'd never let on to Mia that she was looking forward to going.

***

A few hours later, the girls were showered, primped, and heading out the door of Mia's apartment to meet up with Chase. Mia went all out in a *come fuck me* outfit that dripped with thirst and left

not a damn thing to the imagination. She decided on a yellow BCBGeneration wrap short-sleeved romper, which was two sizes too small and barely covered the bottom curve of her ass and should have read *Got Milk* across the chest. Mia paired it with a set of multi-colored Steve Madden Proto-S studded pumps, and added a matching clutch. She opted for a *wet and wavy* look with her Brazilian bundles, and topped her flawless makeup application off with some Dior Couture lip color.

"Damn bitch, this ain't no damn photo shoot!" Kassidy bucked at Mia's over the top outfit for this so-called private party.

"You know how I do girl, flawless every time I step out the door, I don't play. I gotta be ready to roll up on my future husband at any given moment," Mia winked, playfully blowing a kiss in Kassidy's direction as she twerked her booty a few times.

"Uh uh chick, ain't no tellin wheeeeeere those lips been...I'm good," Kassidy giggled.

"Anyway, I know that ain't what you wearing?!" Mia interrupted.

"What's wrong with what I got on? Why am I gonna try to impress a dude I don't even know!"

Going for the opposite of Mia's thirst bucket look, Kassidy opted for a simple look with a pair of white, raw-hemmed, distressed 7 skinny jeans and a Vince Camuto lace-up crop top. Face beat with a nude, natural look, she served up ultra-kissable lips with her MAC Vamplify Lipglass. Having sweated out her silk press earlier that day in yoga class, her natural, wavy curls draped her shoulders and hung loosely down her back.

"And you WON'T know him if he sees you lookin' all basic and shit either–you wanna be the old cat lady with no man and a house full of cats, don't you?" Mia frowned at her friend.

"Girl bye-just 'cuz I don't have all my asssssss-ets out like I'm in a display window don't mean I'm basic. This is what you call *classy*–but you're a rat, so you wouldn't know nothin' 'bout this,"

CHASE & KASSIDY: ALL EYES ON US

Kassidy sassed as she struck a pose, slid her hand down to her hip, and popped her lips at Mia.

"I got ya rat, bourgeois ass heifer," Mia rolled her eyes in return. "Umm, ain't you forgetting something tho?" Mia paused before grabbing her purse and phone from the side table.

"Something like what?" Kassidy inquired.

"Uhh, your keys."

"Nope, I'm not forgetting anything because you're driving!" Kassidy laughed as she headed out the door. Mia playfully huffed before grabbing and digging around in the bottom of her purse, retrieving her keys a few seconds later. *This spoiled ass heifer gets on my nerves sometimes*, Mia thought to herself.

The besties had roughly a 30-minute drive from Mia's spot out in St. George to the park. While Mia chatted away with excitement on what she hoped would be their come up, Kassidy's mind returned to the previous night, and the tingle she'd felt when Chase grazed up against her ass. She wasn't sure what it was about this Chase cat, but he had her intrigued and they hadn't even said two words to each other yet.

Although Kassidy usually dated the uptown, choirboy, vanilla sex-type dudes, a part of her had always secretly longed to see what it was like to kick it with a bad boy–the same kind of dudes her dad swore were nothing but trouble. From his chocolate-dipped complexion to his chiseled jawline and picture-perfect smile, Kassidy was more than curious to see just what Chase had in store. Just then Mia announced their arrival, interrupting Kassidy's daydream.

"Damn that nigga fine as fuck!" Mia exclaimed as they parked and exited her Honda Accord. Kassidy whipped her head around and trained her eyes on Chase, who was several feet down to their right, leaning against his truck with his phone up to his ear.

"Come on girl," Mia came around the car. She nudged Kassidy as her heels assaulted the pavement, anxiously headed in Chase's direction. Kassidy ran a hand through her curls, double-

checked the laces of her crop top, and followed Mia's lead. The closer they got to Chase, the more she felt the butterflies in her stomach dancing in a flurried swarm. *Chill out girl, let Mia do all the clowning,* she silently chided herself as they came within just a few feet of Chase, which was close enough for his Tom Ford Noir to stroke her nostrils.

"Fa sho, hit me later," Chase ended his phone call as they approached, returning his phone to pocket.

"Heyyyy Chase," Mia cooed, reaching her hand out to teasingly tap his arm, like they were old friends.

"What's good ma," Chase chuckled, leaning back against his Denali with his arms folded across his chest. His biceps effortlessly tested the elasticity of the sleeves of his white Armani t-shirt. Joined with a pair of black Armani jeans and a pair of black Timbs, he rounded out his look with a Tag Heuer watch, a white gold diamond rosary, and a set of cube diamond studs that sparkled just as bright as his smile. With next to no effort, this nigga was fine as fuck, and the cocky smirk his face wore was evidence that he knew it.

"Nothin' much, tryin' to see what yo' fine ass has in store for us," Mia beamed. Chase shook his head at Mia for a brief second before shifting his gaze to Kassidy.

"Us...and your friend is..." Chase paused, waiting for Mia's follow-up.

"Oh, my bad, this is my boo Kassidy. Kassidy, this is the king himself, Chase Baptiste." Chase shook his head at Mia's smothering effort at impressing him. *Damn this broad is thirsty as fuck,* he silently mused.

"Kassidy...pretty name ma, nice to meet you," Chase smiled and for the first time, Kassidy was witness to a perfectly identical set of the deepest dimples she'd ever seen. A few of his freshly twisted locks fell across his right shoulder as he extended his hand toward Kassidy.

"Likewise," Kassidy smiled nonchalantly, shaking Chase's massive hand. *Mmm, big hands AND big feet? I bet this nigga is–*

"So where we rollin' to, Chase?" Mia interrupted Chase and Kassidy's stare off; clearly, those two were feeling the fuck out of each other. Chase gave Kassidy another seductive once over, biting the right corner of his bottom lip before responding to Mia.

"Yeah, 'bout that, we're rollin' out to Jersey–ay, thanks for dropping her off tho, I'll make sure she gets home," Chase winked.

"Huh? Wha...what you mean *dropping her off*? You said you were tryin' to get up?" Mia questioned.

"And I did–with Ms. Kassidy. You good tho, 'preciate you bringing her," Chase spoke before returning his attention to Kassidy as if she was a package he had been waiting on from FedEx. "You ready, beautiful?"

"Uhh...ready for what? Umm, I'm not sure if I should..." Kassidy hesitated, suddenly nervous about being alone with Chase. Truthfully, she wouldn't miss Mia's loud ass, but she couldn't help but be somewhat nervous about riding off in a strange car with a guy she just met.

"I got you ma, lemme just take you to dinner and if you want, I'll take you right home after...no pressure, promise?" Chase asked, knowing full well going home would be the last thing she wanted to do by the end of their night.

"Umm...I guess... Mia, are you good?" Kassidy faltered, nervously shifting her weight from one foot to the other. Mia popped her lips and exhaled roughly, visibly irritated that Chase's invitation was really meant for Kassidy.

"I mean yeah, I'm good girl, go get ya grub on. I'll just umm, go home and crash and watch some Netflix or somethin'...not like I got shit else to do tonight all dressed up and shit," Mia flashed a fake smile, even though she was silently cursing Chase for his fraud ass bait and switch.

"Okay, well...call you later?" Kassidy smiled, hoping her friend wasn't too mad that Chase had played her to the left.

"Yeah girl, call me when you're on your way to get your ride from my crib," Mia rolled her eyes, turning to head back to her car.

"Hop in ma," Chase reached out to grab Kassidy's hand; she hesitated at first, but slid her palm into his as he led her to the passenger side of his truck. "You good?" he queried, securing his grasp on her hand as he helped her step up into the vehicle.

"Yup, perfect," Kassidy assured. Chase closed the passenger door, then trotted around the rear of the truck and slid into the driver seat.

Chapter 6

"Nice ride," Kassidy smirked as Chase settled in his seat and turned the ignition over. The exterior of his Denali boasted a modest appearance, in stark contrast to the state-of-the-art interior. Even his vehicle oozed arrogance as nearly every square inch appeared to be custom-made to Chase's specification. His headrests were outfitted with some sort of custom crest or insignia that caught Kassidy's eye.

"So...where are we headed?"

"You got a minute? I mean, can you hang with me for a good minute?" Chase inquired.

"Uhh, sure...what'd you have in mind?"

"Cool cool, wanna take you to my fave spot out in Jersey; is that okay?"

"Jersey? Sure, but this spot must have some damn good food if it calls you all the way from the Island," Kassidy joked.

"No doubt. I'll let you judge for yourself tho," he eyed her briefly before returning his gaze to the in-dash monitor connected to his backup camera; Kassidy returned his smile as she fastened her seatbelt.

"So your accent...you're not from the Island, are you?" Kassidy probed, attempting to strike up a conversation to mask her nervous energy as they headed for the expressway.

"Same thing I was thinking about you, ma; you look more uptown Manhattan. How you wind up down here in the forgotten borough?" Chase joked.

"Uptown?" Kassidy playfully frowned.

"I'm messin' with you, baby girl. But fareal, I'm Staten Island all day. I'm Haitian tho," Chase answered her question.

"Interesting. Means I gotta watch your ass, you might have a voodoo doll tucked away somewhere," Kassidy teased, glancing all around the interior of his truck as though she were checking for any hidden dolls.

"Ahh, I see you got jokes," Chase laughed, "Nah, my moms is old world Haitian, but I'm Staten Island all day. Everybody knows that," Chase explained.

"Hmm, funny…never heard of you before last night," Kassidy smirked, masking her anxiety with a bit of mild sarcasm.

"Cute, sexy, and you got a mouth on you; I dig it," Chase returned her smirk.

Chase and Kassidy fell into a light-hearted conversation the rest of drive to Jersey. By the time they crossed the Outerbridge Crossing, Kassidy felt at ease in Chase's presence, like they'd kicked it plenty of times before. She was so lost in their conversation that she didn't realize they'd arrived at their destination until she saw Chase shift his truck into park and kill the ignition.

"This is it?" Kassidy frowned, looking up at the building just beyond the curb where Chase had just parked; it appeared to be a meager walkup on what was a crowded street that evening.

"Yeah–hold up, lemme get that for you," he interrupted Kassidy as she reached for the door handle. He hopped out his side and jogged around the front end to reach Kassidy's door. He then pulled the door open, catching Kassidy's hand as she swung her legs out, bringing her Bar III platform, peep toe wedges to meet the sidewalk pavement.

"Wow…this is it…" Kassidy reiterated, her face showing her uncertainty at what looked to be a *hole in the wall* eatery. Glancing up at one of the windowpanes, she saw that the place appeared to be called One World, 1 Table.

"I got you, ma. Trust me, the menu won't disappoint," Chase assured her as he armed his alarm, and they made their way to the entrance.

The minute they set foot inside, they were met with a mouth-watering aroma that smelled like a perfect fusion of Caribbean and Spanish food. Reading the look of shock on Kassidy's face, Chase spoke her thoughts.

"Weren't expecting this when you saw the outside, huh?"

"Okay, now I know it's all ladylike to eat like a bird on a first date, but I'm letting you know now that I'm about to pig out," Kassidy spoke, eyes still bucked at all the tasty offerings on the menu. "How did you find this place? I've never even heard of it–and wow, is that *Lanbi an Sòs Lanbi Kreyol* on the menu?!" Kassidy exclaimed.

"Baby girl, what you know 'bout Haitian food?"

"You just watch me chow down and find out," Kassidy winked.

Finding a table off in the corner, Chase pulled Kassidy's chair out and made sure she was seated, then joined her in the seat across the table. The waitress quickly came and took their food and drink orders, promising to return shortly.

"So beautiful, how does a woman like you end up with a friend like Mia?" Chase asked, leaning back and settling in his chair as he locked his fingers and rested his hands along the edge of the table. Kassidy feigned a frown before responding.

"What, you don't like my bestie?"

"I mean, she just seems so...opposite of you," he jeered, locking eyes with her across the table.

"You mean so...thirsty?" Kassidy joked. "But no, she's a cool chick for real. Y'all just don't get to see her like I do."

Just then, the waitress returned with their drinks, and their food followed a short time later. True to her word, Kassidy devoured her food, and snagged a few bites of Chase's order of Griyo and pikliz. The two fell into an easy conversation and as the time seemed to fly, Kassidy marveled at how he seemed to be the perfect gentleman–far from the bossed up street thug that Mia built him up to be. It didn't hurt that the way his accent punctuated his every word kept the throbbing between her thighs going strong the entire time.

"Damn ma, you wasn't playing about grubbing I see. Where it all go tho? Look like you be dodging real food, I almost thought you were one of them bean sprout chicks," he mocked.

Kassidy giggled as she wiped her mouth with her napkin, and took a sip out of her unsweetened iced tea to wash her food down.

"I guess that's your version of a compliment, so I'll take it," Kassidy playfully huffed as she narrowed her eyes at Chase. "I told you, I don't bird peck at food, I eat," she continued.

"It's all gravy baby, and I definitely meant that as a compliment," he flirted as he gave Kassidy an *I want to throw your ass across this table and fuck you 'til the Pope hears your screams* gaze.

Kassidy stared back as she slightly leaned her head to the side. Her legs clasped tightly together as she smiled with her exotic eyes. Her heart began to flutter as her kitty purred with excitement. *Down girl*, she inwardly tried to calm herself from the heat that exchanged each time their eyes met. Chase appreciated that she wasn't all on the dick from jump; he was down for the *chase,* because he was confident that the prize would be his in the end. He continued to get lost in Kassidy's bedroom eyes, silently wondering how cute her fuck faces were. There was no denying that the sexual tension between the two of them was evident. If gasoline would have dripped on the table, the entire restaurant would have gone up in flames. Kassidy was turned on by Chase just as much as he was turned on by her.

Passing on dessert, Chase called for the waitress to bring the check and once he paid, the pair made their way out the exit and back to Chase's truck.

"So this spot was very nice, but you really drive all the way out to Jersey just for the food? All those spots we got on the Island?" Kassidy probed, settling into her seat as she sucked her stomach in, hoping she didn't look like the pig she felt like in that moment. Chase turned the engine over, latched his seatbelt, and disengaged the emergency break before turning to face her with a reply.

"Ma, where you buy your shoes at?"

"Huh? What do you mean?" Kassidy puzzled.

"I mean...what's the first place that pops in your head when you need a new pair of shoes?"

"Umm, Macy's, Neiman's, some place like that, why?"

"How many Payless or Rack Room Shoes, or Shoe Carnivals are there on the Island?"

"Uhh, probably quite a few, I don't know, why?" Kassidy countered, confused as to where Chase was going with his interrogation.

"So quite a few, yet you pass 'em to get to Neiman's, why is that?"

"Cuz I don't do cheap."

"Exactly–quality over quantity, ma," Chase smiled and winked before merging into traffic and leading them back to the Expressway.

Wonder what kinda quality D he got in them Armani's, Kassidy smiled, lost in her X-rated thoughts of who she hoped would be her future thugged-out bad boy.

Chapter 7

Chase and Kassidy pulled up in front of Mia's house to pick up her car, and she noticed Mia's Honda Accord wasn't there. The outside light was on but from the looks of it, Mia had made plans of her own. Kassidy glanced over at Chase, secretly not wanting to end their night, but was glad she decided to listen to Mia and meet up with him at the park.

Easing up right behind Kassidy's car, Chase shifted his truck into park and sat back all cool, calm, and collected as he reclined in his leather seat. He gave Kassidy a sinful leer and she smiled in return, her gaze drenched with lust. Kassidy scooted closer to the armrest and leaned in, offering Chase a cozy embrace; he leaned up to hug her back as the tip of his nose brushed against her neck, and he inhaled a whiff of her Neroli Portofino by Tom Ford. *Damn ma, you so fucking sexy. Bet you taste as good as you smell,* Chase thought to himself.

"Thanks for dinner," she whispered in his ear.

"Pleasure was all mine, beautiful," Chase replied.

Not wanting him to leave her personal space, Kassidy slowly pulled away from Chase as she took one last stare and attempted to get out of the car.

"Hold up baby girl, lemme get that," Chase interjected as he reached for his door handle to walk around and open her door.

"No, it's fine, I got it," Kassidy smiled, opening the door for herself; she stepped onto the pavement of the driveway and walked up to her car. Chase watched as Kassidy hopped in her ride, then shifted into reverse and pulled out of the driveway, making way for her to pull out as well; he stayed and waited until she pulled off as they ended their close-to-perfect date, and finally parted ways.

Chase and Kassidy didn't make any plans to see each other again, but she was definitely looking forward to the next invite; in fact, she fantasized about what it would be like. Chase was more than what she expected, and everything that she wanted. Judging a book by its cover was definitely a mistake in his case, because he was the perfect gentleman, and she was glad she took the chance to see him in a different light. If Kassidy was honest with herself, she didn't want the night to end, but she also didn't want to come off as just another thirsty female who was trying to get next to him; that was the only reason she didn't invite him to follow her back to her place. *Damn sure ain't tryin' to be another Mia*, Kassidy smiled to herself.

On her drive home, Kassidy seized her cell phone from her clutch and dialed Mia.

"Yo, where you at? When I got to your crib, your car said look for me," Kassidy questioned.

"What's up girl. I um...I'm with a friend."

"Heifer I thought you said you didn't have plans and you was going home to watch Netflix."

"Well I did, and then a bitch got bored so I rode through DeMarco's."

"DeMarco? Don't even get me started on him. Anyhoo...I thought you said you wasn't feeling him anymore? As soon as I leave your ass unattended, you go making booty calls with exes."

DeMarco was Mia's ex. A while back, the police kicked his door in with a warrant, searching for drugs when Mia was over one day. DeMarco was a snake though, and very much bitch made, so he wouldn't dream of going down for charges when he could pin them on someone else; instead, he tried to convince the police that the drugs belonged to Mia. DeMarco was a convicted felon, and he thought if Mia took the charge, he wouldn't have to go back to prison. Mia was hopelessly in love with DeMarco, but not stupid enough to go to jail for anyone. To Mia's dismay, she still went to

jail that day, along with DeMarco. Fortunately, her lawyer got her off and all charges against her were dropped. DeMarco had to do his time and was mad at Mia for not taking the fall. He thought if Mia loved him enough, she could do him that one favor, being that it would have been her first offense. Mia thought DeMarco had lost his damn mind, and no dick on Earth was good enough to sit behind bars for. Thinking back on their stormy past, Kassidy scratched her head as she wondered how her friend could be dickmatized by such a clown.

"Girl, I couldn't have said it better myself. It's all your fault," Mia laughed as she tried to disguise her and Kassidy's conversation in front of her ex, DeMarco. "Enough about that...so what happened with ole boy? Did he fuck your brains out?"

Kassidy laughed. "No silly, but the date went well. Definitely not what I expected."

"I told you. See...maybe next time when I tell you something you'll just take my word for it the first time instead of giving me the runaround."

"Okay Mia–since you need to hear it. My bad chica, you were right. Chase Baptiste is all that you said he was; shit, even more."

Mia laughed. "Uh huh...lemme find out somebody catching feelings. Hmm...if he's all that I heard he was, wait until he slides in-between them thighs. Maybe he already has from the sound of it," Mia teased.

"Girl I did not fuck that man; shit, I barely know him. And who catching feelings? I just said the date went well. That's it."

"Yeah mmm hmm...tell that shit to somebody who don't know your ass."

"Shouldn't you be screaming to the top of your lungs right about now anyway? Bye, get off my phone."

"I did...right before you called. I'll hit you back in the a.m. though."

"Not so fast, trick. Don't tell me you're sleeping over there, Mia?"

"Umm maybe."

"Mia...you know that nigga don't mean you no good, especially after what he did to you. Okay...if you're still not over the dick and you wanted to fuck him, then fuck him–but leave it at that. Take your ass home and make him work to get you back. If you ask me, that sorry ass nigga doesn't deserve you anyway."

"See...you know you can't leave me alone and you are absolutely right. I will definitely do that. The nightstand has already been compensated anyway."

"...and I expect no less from you," Kassidy shook her head and chuckled at her free-spirited friend, "Love you chica, and call me to let me know you made it home safe. Orrr...you can just shoot a text."

"Alright boo. Love you more, muah," Mia said as she pouted her lips to give Kassidy an air kiss through the phone.

Kassidy and Mia ended their conversation and Mia got up and left, just as she told Kassidy she would.

Chapter 8

A couple of weeks had passed, and other than a few short texts here and there, Chase and Kassidy hadn't seen or spoken to one another. Kassidy was over at her parents, and her dad Kameron was grilling her about school and getting her life together again. They had Sunday family dinners, and Kassidy would always stop by to put in family time with her parents and siblings. That was Kassidy's way of staying family-oriented, just the way her parents brought her up to be. This Sunday was no different as they all sat at the dinner table, and everyone was quiet except the head honcho Kameron. When he spoke, everyone else took notice.

"Listen...no disrespect Dad, but I didn't come here to get grilled yet again. I came to have dinner," Kassidy grumbled in an easy tone as she continued to chew on her food; her father's interrogation was beginning to irritate her. *Damn...this nigga ain't got no chill, for real man. He acts like I'm out here selling pussy or something,* Kassidy mulled to herself.

"Well maybe if you would just stop bullshitting around and get your ass back into school, we wouldn't have to have this kind of conversation at dinner," Kameron roared, frustrated with his daughter's indifference at thinking about her future.

"That's enough Kameron! Must we do this every Sunday? Leave the girl alone," Kassidy's mom Maria snapped as she got up and started to clear the dinner table. She knew that she could always count on her husband to disturb the peace of any family gathering by making yet another move to try to control their oldest daughter's life.

Kassidy looked at her father, and resentment started to replace the unconditional love she'd held for him since she was a little girl. Her father's constant school demands were the last thing she wanted to hear at Sunday dinner. As a little girl, Kassidy was under a spell at her daddy's every word, but he now failed to realize that she wasn't that same little girl anymore that he tucked in bed at

night. Kassidy still loved her dad, but his meddling with her life was overbearing and no longer welcomed.

"Maybe if you left your work at work and stopped bringing it home and handling me like I'm one of them dudes on the street that you lock up, then maybe we could sit at the dinner table like normal people. Have you ever even taken the time to ask me what my plans were for my life instead of pushing your plans on me?" Kassidy seethed, growing a serious set of balls as she challenged her father.

"I've worked my ass off day and night to make sure this family had everything. I give you all damn near everything you could ever want or need, and how do you repay me...by pissing away my hard-earned money that I paid towards tuition and dropping out of school–and I'm supposed to give a rat's ass about what you may *think* you want to do? You will do what I tell you to do," Kameron growled as his fiery eyes scalded Kassidy.

As if it sensed she needed an escape from her father's badgering, her phone rang. She looked down at the number and didn't recognize it, but was curious to know who it was–anything to get out of the uncomfortable, yet repetitive conversation she was having with her father.

"Excuse me, but I gotta take this," Kassidy sighed as she got up from the table.

"Is that phone call more important than what I'm saying right now!" Kameron boomed.

Kassidy looked over at her father, but continued to remove herself from the table. She walked out the dining room and entered the kitchen.

"Hello," she answered with a soft tone that bubbled over with her annoyance at her father and his cavalier temper.

"What's up ma?"

"Who is this?" Kassidy answered as her annoyance rocketed.

"Your man."

"My *man*? I didn't know I had one," Kassidy sucked her teeth as a leer stole across her face when she recognized the man's

voice. Her cheeks flushed in a rosy shade, and her heart fluttered with excitement.

"Well you do now. Where you at, ma?"

"Oh, so nowwww you have time to call, Mr. I'm So Busy," Kassidy feigned irritation at not having heard from Chase sooner.

"Nah, it's not even like that baby girl, business keeps me busy...so where you at?"

"Um...at my parents but I'm about to leave here in a few minutes. Why, wassup?"

"I'm just tryin' to find out what time my woman is gonna fall through and chill wit a nigga tonight?"

"Oh you just have it all figured out, don't you?" Kassidy's lips formed a wide smile, reflecting her amusement and intrigue at Chase's take charge attitude. *This nigga cocky as hell.*

"No doubt, so I'm gonna see you tonight, right?" Chase reaffirmed.

Having had enough of the all-knowing Kameron Kingston for the night, Kassidy figured she'd entertain Chase's little request, even if he did have a fucked up way of asking. "Umm yeah, when?"

"You said you're about to leave, right?"

"Yeah, I did. Where?"

"Anywhere you want, ma."

What's that supposed to mean? "Um...okay. We'll meet me at my place. I'll text you the address when I'm on my way there."

"Aight. See you in a lil bit."

"Okay," Kassidy answered as she looked down at the phone and smiled.

Chase's call briefly took Kassidy's mind off her father's bitching about what all he had done for the family, as well as his domineering opinions on her decision to take a break from school. Just as she inwardly felt relief at her reprieve, her mother walked in.

"Are you okay, baby?" Maria asked as she laid her hand on top of Kassidy's arm.

"Yeah Mom, I'm fine. I just wish Daddy would lay off me about school. It's getting old. It's not that I'm not ever going back, I just felt like I needed a break from school to get my mind together, so I took one," Kassidy explained as she stood with her arms crossed in front of her.

"It's okay, baby. You have the right to take a break if you choose to. It's your life."

"Yeah I know; I just wish Daddy knew that."

"Don't worry, I'll talk to him."

"Thanks, Mom," Kassidy smiled as she leaned in, falling into her mother's warm embrace. "Mom, I'm gonna head out...I'm not sure if I'll come over next Sunday. I can't take much more of Dad and his interrogations; I just don't want to be harassed about school every time I set foot through the door."

"KK, please try not to take your father's concern as him not loving you or wanting what's best for you. And please, don't stop coming over because of a disagreement you all may be having," Kassidy's mother begged of her as she let out an exasperated sigh, taking her mother's request into consideration.

"Okay, I'll think about it–but no promises. I just need a break from it all, and Daddy is tap dancing on my last nerve, which isn't helping me focus on what I wanna do at all."

"I understand and as I said, I'll talk to him. Maybe I can get him to back off a bit."

"That would be great. I'll call you soon, okay?"

"Okay, baby," Maria grinned as she leaned in and gave her daughter another hug.

Returning to the dining room, Kassidy found her father still sitting at the table, waiting for her return. He had something to say, and he waited for her to finish her phone call so he could say it.

"I'm leaving, Dad. I'll see you later," Kassidy announced as she stood by the dinner table.

"We are not finish talking, Kassidy. It's rude to just leave in the middle of having dinner with your family. We raised you better than that."

Kassidy inhaled and exhaled again. She closed her eyes and slightly raised her head to the ceiling. She took in a few breaths to try to calm herself down before she said something to her father that she would later regret.

"Dad, I have to go. We will finish this conversation another time, okay?"

BAM.

Kameron slammed his palms onto the table. The loud sound sent Maria storming out of the kitchen, and back into the dining room. "Amelia and Geno, give your sister and I some privacy," Kameron dismissed Kassidy's younger brother and sister as crinkles took up residence in his forehead. He then pointed to the stairs, signaling them to go to their rooms.

"But Dad, I'm still eating," Amelia whined.

"Now!" Kameron's outburst startled Amelia and Geno, as well as Kassidy. The thunder in their father's voice intimidated them all.

"Kam...don't you think you're being unreasonable. I mean...the kids are still eating. You and Kassidy can finish your conversation later."

"Stay out of this, Maria. This is between Kassidy and myself."

"She's my daughter too Kameron, and you are being unreasonably ridiculous."

Maria wouldn't normally defy her husband, especially not in front of their children, but she too had grown tired of Kameron trying to control what Kassidy did and didn't do. Kassidy just stood there. She wasn't sure if she should stick around or continue with her original plans to leave. Her father hardly ever raised his voice at her, so she knew he must have been really upset.

"Dad..."

"I will do the talking–you just listen. Sit down, now," Kameron demanded as he pointed to a seat at the end of the table.

Kassidy looked at her father, his enraged eyes now filled with disappointment. She knew in that moment that if she didn't stand her ground, her father would forever treat her like the kid he thought she still was. Her hazel eyes began to pool with tears, and it took every fiber in her being to trust herself and not let her father continue to muscle her decisions.

"I'll see you next week, Daddy," she said as she walked off and went to the living room, headed out the front door.

"Kassidy!" Kameron yelled as he watched her walk away, but she ignored her father and kept walking.

Kassidy sat in her car and rested her head on the steering wheel. She hated to disrespect her father, but she didn't have the energy to continue to talk about school anymore. Her salty tears hit the steering wheel, and she wept for a minute. She finally pulled herself together, raised her head, and started her car. She pulled out of her parents' driveway and headed home with a heavy heart.

Chapter 9

Thirty minutes later, Kassidy was pulling into her garage and relieved to finally be at home. Dropping her mail, keys, and purse on an end table, Kassidy kicked her shoes off and fell into the plush, welcoming embrace of her overstuffed sofa. *Damn I forgot to text Chase the address. My daddy know he did a number on me today,* Kassidy thought to herself as she stretched to grab her purse from the end table, dug her phone out, and texted Chase her address. He quickly replied, and Kassidy smiled at how eager he seemed to spend some time with her.

CHASE: *thought u forgot*

KASSIDY: *Never*

CHASE: *wrappin' some stuff up, be there shortly. Can't wait to c u*

KASSIDY: *Take your time, can't wait 2 c my man either*

Kassidy smiled to herself, thinking about how Chase had told her that he was her man earlier.

CHASE: *Mmm, like the way that sounds. One*

"Shit, I guess I should shower before he gets here. I smell like outside," Kassidy shrugged as she dipped into the shower and bathed herself with Victoria's Secret Pure Seduction. She lathered herself from head to toe, rinsed clean, and then got out of the shower and dried herself off. She slipped into a breezy summer dress that caressed her slender curves perfectly. Kassidy figured she'd go with a more subtle look as opposed to dramatic or seductive, being that she was already comfortable and it would be Chase's first time in her home. She let her naturally body-waved curls air dry and swiped a bubble gum color gloss across her lips that complemented her skin tone. She slid her feet into her flat Bebe sandals as the ribbon laced around the bottom part of her slender legs.

Just as she gave herself a once over in her full-length mirror, the doorbell rang. *Oh shit... he's here. Damn...I thought I would have*

more time. Kassidy gave herself one last cursory inspection, ran her fingers through her hair, and made a popping sound with her lips, which was her way of making sure the gloss was dispersed evenly across her lips. She left out of her bedroom and walked through the hallway, arriving at her front door a few seconds later. She peeked out of the oval glass pane of the door and seen that it was Chase. Placing her hand on the brass knob, she sucked in a deep breath. Kassidy opened the door and there he was, the object of her desire standing there looking like a life-sized block of dark chocolate, begging to melt in her mouth.

"Hey, you found it huh? Was it hard?"

"No, not at all. You know I got GPS, so I'll never have a problem finding my way to you. Stick with me and I'll teach you how to never doubt ya man," Chase grinned as Kassidy creamed at his beautiful smile.

"Is that right?" Kassidy continued to smile as the *I'm your man* saying had quickly become their little thing. "Come on in, silly," she said as she opened the door wider, granting Chase entrance.

Standing inside the opened doorway, Chase paused and stepped closer to Kassidy; he leaned down, stopping just inches short of Kassidy's lips. Locking eyes with her as she nervously gnawed away at her bottom lip, he pressed his lips into hers in a soft kiss. Hesitating for a moment, Kassidy was caught off guard by his forward gesture; she thought he would give her a hug, but not a kiss when he saw her. Breaking their kiss, Kassidy stared passionately into Chase's eyes and leaned back to continue their kiss, their tongues playing follow the leader as they swirled in a cyclone of exchanged saliva. Chase backed her up against the door and continued to plunge his tongue down her throat, sucking the bubble gum gloss off her lips as she breathed *fuck me now* into his mouth.

Ohhhh fuck, what are you doing to me Chase, Kassidy inwardly gasped as her fountain began to flow and her breathing grew heavy. "Hold up, wait...wait...wait..." she whispered.

"Mmm, I been wanting to do that from the moment I saw you at the club," Chase mumbled in her ear. *Damn, you always smell so fucking good. I can't wait to get in that pussy.*

"Umm, can we get out of the door, please?"

"Oh...my bad ma," Chase lightly chortled as he took his hand and fondled her breast. "Damn...you making this hard for a nigga...I don't want to stop."

"Then don't," Kassidy whispered.

Chase slid his tongue back in her mouth, and took her long legs and wrapped them around him as he scooped her ass up and away from her spot against the door. Kassidy hugged Chase around the shoulder and neck as she continued to twirl her tongue around in his mouth; she hungrily sucked his tongue, which tasted like he invented sex. Chase shut the door with his foot and carried Kassidy to her couch, laying her down before gliding on top of her. She seductively eased her legs open, granting Chase entry to press his body into hers and awaken his manhood, which was ready and eager to put in some work. Chase trailed his hand underneath her dress, embarking on a flirtatious exploration of *his woman's* body.

"Damn girl, you so wet."

"Mmm....sssss," Kassidy uttered as Chase's fingertips made circular motions around her clit.

"No panties either?" Chased teased as he slid his middle finger deep into her wetness, his other fingers folded forward. He pushed in and pulled out, in and out as Kassidy continued to moan.

"Mmmm...come...let's," Kassidy began, "let's go to my bedroom."

Removing his finger, Chase slid his hand down Kassidy's milky smooth thigh and stood up. He reached his hand out to her, peeling her from the couch. Placing her hand into his, she attempted to lead the way to her bedroom.

"Wait..." Kassidy said as she hesitated to go to the bedroom. She took a deep breath and shut her eyes for a split second.

"What's wrong, ma?"

"I umm...it's just...I don't think I'm ready for this right now. My mind is running a million miles a minute...it's just too soon...I mean...I just think we should..." Kassidy hesitated, nervously biting her bottom lip.

"Stop thinking and just go with the flow, ma," Chase teased.

Kassidy gave him the side eye. She wanted Chase just as much as he wanted her, but she didn't want to be just another woman that he had slept with. She had no interest whatsoever in being *friends with benefits* and definitely wasn't into him leaving money on the nightstand, as Mia would have suggested. As much as Chase had her body on fire, Kassidy's mind was still in a fog after the blow up with her father earlier that evening. It weighed heavy on her, and she was feeling a little guilty about walking away and not finishing their conversation.

"Imma pretend that you didn't just say that."

"Aw lighten up; I'm just fucking with you. Listen ma...I don't want you to do anything that you're not ready or comfortable doing," Chase said as he grabbed her hand and led her back to the couch. "I always want my woman to give herself willingly...so I can devour her shit like there's no tomorrow," Chase joked, trying to lighten the mood a little. "For real though baby girl, what's wrong? I noticed something in your voice when I spoke to you earlier. I was in the middle of something, and that's why I didn't address it then," Chase continued, patting his lap as a beckon for Kassidy to join him; she took a seat and leaned back into his chest, then took a deep breath again before replying.

"Ahhh...nothing really. It's just...when I was over at my parents' earlier, my dad and I kinda got into it. We don't normally do that, but he's really tripping about me taking some time off from college, and he wants to micromanage all of my decisions. I'm just tired of it, really."

"College? So you're in school?"

"Yeah...well, actually I was, but I'm taking some time off to figure out what I really want to do, instead of just doing what my

father thinks I should do," Kassidy lightly chuckled. "Actually, he had the audacity to tell me I *better* do what he wants. Can you believe that?"

"Wow...Pops ain't playing witcha, huh?" Chased teased.

"You have no idea," Kassidy sighed, lightly laughing.

"Do you think your Pops loves you?"

"Yes, of course I do. I know he loves me."

"Well as a man, just know he has his daughter's best interest at heart. So don't take it personal. I'm sure he means well. He's just being a father."

If a pin would have dropped, it would have made a loud bang because of the quietness that swallowed the room. Kassidy thought about what Chase said for a minute, even though she still had her own reservations about what her father was doing to her.

Needing a mental break, Kassidy shifted the direction of the conversation all together and asked Chase if he had kids, and what his dreams and aspirations were. Chase told her he was far from a college prep boy, and that he was content with being self-made. He also asked her what her future plans were, and whether she planned on going back to school or not. The two became more acquainted, and their conversation became light and funny. They laughed at each other's jokes and made plans to see each other again. Chase didn't pressure Kassidy for sex, although he wanted to get balls deep in the pussy. He respected her changing her mind as they were headed to the bedroom earlier, and didn't even bring the situation up. Chase was feeling Kassidy and didn't want to scare her off with his usual aggressiveness, so he took it easy and treated her like the jewel she was. *His jewel.*

Chapter 10

Over the next two months, Chase and Kassidy got more familiar and hung out whenever Chase wasn't jetting off to St. Louis or up and down the East Coast. As much as Kassidy wanted to hold back and avoid anything too serious with Chase, she felt herself falling for him more and more with each day that passed. He dominated her thoughts and made it even more difficult for her to give any amount of thought to what she planned to do with her future.

Kameron continued his attempts to exert his overbearing authority on Kassidy, demanding that she at least get a job while she played ex-student turned couch potato. Kassidy, however, was determined to stand her ground and politely dismissed her dad's slick comments–until he cut her off financially, at least.

Freshly showered from her morning run, Kassidy plopped down on her couch and cracked open a bottle as she grabbed her iPad. She'd been so preoccupied with Chase the past few months that she'd let her reading addiction fall off. Swiping to her Kindle app, she picked up right where she left off with *Sky & Sincere 2: His Rider, Her Roller* by MyKisha Mac. Kassidy got lost in the book for a brief moment, all wrapped up in Sincere and his bossed up moves. *Sincere is bae all day long...that nigga can DEFINITELY get it,* Kassidy mused to herself. As always, Chase's infectious smile interrupted her thoughts, and she couldn't help but to think about how Chase was her Sincere. *Her roller.* They might not have declared anything official, but Chase had her heart, hands down–the same way that she was almost certain she had his.

Just as her mind began to drift to visions of scraping her nails along what she was certain would be Chase's super toned back, Omeeka's song "All Eyes On You" rapped to her from her cell phone.

Got the club goin' crazy

All these hittas, but my eyes on you
Is you somebody's baby?

Seeing her mother's incoming call, she smiled and eagerly swiped right to answer the call, her mother's jovial voice instantly flooding her ear.

"Hey baby!" Maria greeted her daughter.

"Hey Mom, what are you up to today?" Kassidy beamed; her mother was the light of her life, and she loved the way she always accepted her and let her be her own woman.

"Oh the usual, but I should be asking you that question–you sound like you're on cloud nine over there. What's the tea girlie, spill it!"

"What? Ma, I don't know what you're talkin' about. I'm just having a good day, is that allowed?" Kassidy smiled even wider, amazed at how her mother always seemed to hit the nail on the head with her.

"KK look, I birthed you, so even on your best day, you're not going to get one over on me. Now what's his name?" Maria playfully demanded.

Damn, how she know, Kassidy paused for a second, shocked again that her mom was dead on. "What makes you think there's a guy involved? Maybe I'm just–"

"Little girl, save it for the funny papers, a woman knows–so who is he?"

Realizing her attempts to mask her joy were futile, Kassidy gave her mom the cliff notes version of her situationship with Chase. After grilling her for not mentioning Chase sooner, Maria let Kassidy know that she wanted to meet him ASAP.

"Bring him to dinner on Sunday, that way we can all meet him."

"Wait a minute Mom, you know good and well that I am not about to bring a guy to dinner and have King Kingston slaughter him at the table. No ma'am."

"KK relax, I'll handle your father, he'll be on his best behavior," her mother reassured her.

"Yeah right–you *do* know who your husband is right? Best behavior? Tuh. I'll believe that when I see it–don't worry, I'll wait."

"Baby listen, everything will be fine. So I'll see you and him Sunday. Muah, love you baby doll!" her mother exclaimed before disconnecting the call, leaving Kassidy's bottom lip in limbo.

***

Sunday came quicker than expected, and to say that Kassidy was nervously anxious would be an understatement. While it was always a treat to be in Chase's presence, she couldn't ignore the dread that she felt in the pit of her stomach as she thought about how her father would react to Chase. After her mother's phone call, she psyched herself into inviting Chase to Sunday dinner with her parents, even though she knew there was a strong possibility that the big bad wolf, Kameron Kingston, would start in on her again–a conversation she was less than enthused to have. Maria convinced her daughter that daddy dearest would be on his best behavior, but Kassidy still had her doubts; however, she didn't allow it to stop her from inviting Chase over. She knew her mother wanted to meet the man in her life, and Kassidy wanted her to meet Chase as well. There was nothing like mommy's stamp of approval about the guy who she hoped would soon be *her man*.

"Hey babe, where you at? Remember I told you about dinner with my parents tonight?"

"Damn...that's right. Um...what time is it gonna be again, bae?"

"Six o'clock–don't tell me you forgot, Chase?" Kassidy uttered, slightly irritated but realizing she only told him once on Wednesday when they spent the day together.

"Nah, I didn't forget about the dinner but honestly, I did forget about the time with you tempting and teasing me; walking around in them lil bitty ass shorts and shit. You know you could have got it, right?" Chase flirted.

"Maybe you should have just given it to me," Kassidy teased.

"Hmm, now you tell me," he laughed. "Hey...can I just meet you there? I mean...will that be okay? I'm kind of tied up right now, and I really need to handle something before I take off for the rest of the night."

"Um...I guess it shouldn't be a problem...although I thought we would ride together..." Kassidy said with a saddened tone.

"Don't be like that, ma. You know it ain't even like that. I'm coming, promise. If I don't do anything else today, meeting your parents is definitely on my agenda," Chase said as he thought about how meeting Kassidy's parents was a sure way to get closer to her.

Kassidy smiled through the phone. "Okay, I will hold you to that."

"Text me the address."

"Done."

"Aight. See you later. One."

Chase hung up the phone, and Kassidy grabbed her keys and headed to her parents.

Chapter 11

Kassidy pulled up in front of her parents' home, and her mother met her at the door; anxious at her arrival, Maria couldn't wait to see who this young man was that had captured her daughter's attention. Kassidy smiled and shook her head when she noticed her mother, who was standing in the door and squinting her eyes, trying to see if there was someone else in the car with her.

This lady is a mess. Just couldn't wait. I see you, Mom.

Kassidy honked her horn to playfully pester her mother as she stood waving at her. Maria closed her hands in front of her as if she was saying a prayer. She didn't meddle in Kassidy's life the way Kameron did, but after her phone call with her daughter, she knew that there had to be someone special in her life. She could sense Kassidy's upbeat energy through the phone, and when she heard the cheerful shift in Kassidy's mood when she mentioned that there had to be a man in her life, Maria was certain her daughter was under the influence of a new love, even though Kassidy denied it.

Kassidy parked and got out of the car. Her mother stood there looking and waiting for the other door to open, but it never did. Her facial expression changed from happy to confused, because Kassidy told her she would bring a date to dinner.

"It's okay, he'll be joining us later. You can get back to your happy place," Kassidy teased as she walked up the stairs and gave her mother a big hug.

"Hey baby, it's always good to see you. So you say your friend will be joining us later? Is everything okay?"

"Yeah, everything's fine. He just got caught up..." Kassidy paused. "Um...caught up at work. Yeah, he got caught up at the workplace and will be here in a little bit."

"I see. You never said what he does."

Kassidy smiled. "Geez...can we at least get inside first? You're starting to sound just like someone else I know," Kassidy teased as her mother laughed.

"Sure baby, we can go inside," Maria said as she turned around and walked inside. Kassidy followed her to the dining room.

"Where's Dad?" Kassidy said as she noticed her father wasn't sitting at the table or anywhere in sight.

"Oh, your father's just finishing up getting ready upstairs. He should be done in a minute."

"KK!" Amelia said as she ran and gave Kassidy a tight hug.

"Hey my baby," Kassidy gleamed as she bent down and picked Amelia up. Amelia was six, the baby of the bunch and Geno was eight, the middle child; Kassidy was the oldest of them all.

"Where's Geno?" Kassidy asked as he came out of the game room from playing with his Xbox.

"Hey KK."

"What up dude?" Kassidy said as she gave Geno a hug.

Just as Kassidy began to playfully wrestle with her brother, her father made his grand entrance.

"Geno, what did I tell you about playing around the dinner table?" Kameron halted their horseplay.

"Aww Dad relax, we were just playing around," Kassidy chuckled, hoping to lighten the eerily tense mood that entered the room with her father.

"Playing around–that's something you know all too well, right?"

"So how about we all get seated so we can dig in!" Maria interjected, shutting Kameron's sarcastic jab down before he could get started.

"Mommyyyyy, we can't eat yet! We have to wait for KK's boyyyyyyfriend," Amelia playfully cooed, shooting a goofy smile Kassidy's way.

"He's nooooot my boyfriend, cutie pie," Kassidy returned the goofy expression.

"Then what do I need to meet him for?" Kameron quipped.

Good ol' Kameron turnt up already; gonna be a long dinner, Kassidy groaned to herself. Just as she heavily exhaled the beginnings of her frustration, the doorbell rang.

"I'll get it!" Maria jumped up, eagerly heading to the front door.

"I'll come with you," Kassidy added, welcoming the break from her dad's piercing gaze. She quickened her steps to beat her mother to the door.

"Hey you," Kassidy smiled as she swung the storm door open.

"Hey beautiful," Chase greeted, leaning down to briefly hug Kassidy before she pulled away and turned to her mother.

"Mom, this is my friend Chase. Chase, this is my mother–"

"Mrs. Kingston. It's such a pleasure to meet you. I see where Kassidy gets those top model looks from. Thanks so much for inviting me into your home," Chase smiled as he drew Maria's hand into a gentle handshake; his charm was in overdrive as he worked to win Kassidy's mom over.

"Ohhhh Chase, so nice to meet you!" Maria beamed, taking in Chase's clean-cut appearance as he stood before her in designer khakis, an Armani button-down shirt, and Armani loafers.

Come come, dinner awaits!" Maria ushered the two in and towards the dining room. Kameron rose from the table the minute they entered the room, certain that his eyes were playing tricks on him. *It can't be,* he thought to himself.

"Uhhh Daddy, this is Chase. He's a really good friend of mine." Kassidy hoped her voice didn't betray the bundle of nerves she felt at that moment. Kameron stood glaring at Chase, arms folded across his chest as he and Chase's eyes locked in a menacing stare.

"Got a last name, son?" Kameron spat.

"Baptiste. Chase Baptiste." Chase maintained eye contact with Kameron, inwardly amused at what he detected was Kameron's rising anger at his presence.

"Okayyy, now that we've gotten that out of the way...can we eat?" Kassidy requested, trying to downplay the tension in the room and get past another Kameron Kingston *Officer of the Law* interrogations.

"Uhh, let's all sit while the food's nice and hot," Maria announced, sensing the nonverbal heat exchanged between the two men.

As everyone got seated and began passing the serving dishes around, Kameron's glare never left Chase's face. Kassidy noticed the clenching of Chase's jaw, and her eyes quickly darted up to observe the tense visual standoff between him and her father. She gave his hand a gentle squeeze under the table, and he returned the sentiment as his jaw relaxed. Amelia and Geno were too young to pick up the strained vibe in the room because their father's behavior was the norm around the house, and they expected nothing different from him. Marie watched Kameron, hoping he didn't run Kassidy off yet again as they tried to get past another uncomfortable Sunday dinner–thanks to her husband.

"So sweetie, have you given any thought to the job offer your father proposed to you yet?" Maria posed, hoping to shift Kameron's focus away from harassing Chase.

Kassidy gave her mother the evil stare. She expected that kind of question from her father, not her mother–the one who was always on her side. Maria shrugged her shoulders as she realized what slipped out of her mouth, recognizing her failed attempt to kill the awkwardness that was suffocating the room at the dinner table.

"Uhhh... yeah actually, I did," Kassidy replied with a counterfeit smile, ducking her head into her plate as she stuffed a piece of the dinner roll into her mouth. Chase squeezed her thigh under the table. He could tell the question made Kassidy

uncomfortable, especially after everything she had shared with him about her father being on her back about school.

"Speaking of *jobs*, what line of work are you in, Chase?" Kameron went right in for the kill.

"I work in real estate."

"Do you now? Interesting…so, you're an agent…you sell houses…" Kameron rebutted.

"Actually, I own the firm…so I guess you could say that I have people that sell houses for me," Chase lobbed back, holding his own. Reading Kassidy's nervous frown, he gave her hand a reassuring squeeze under the table.

"So I suppose you do quite a bit of *flipping* and make quite a few *connects,* I mean connections in real estate, huh?" Kameron taunted. "How many *runners*, I mean agents do you have on staff at your umm…firm?"

"I prefer to focus on *new territory* instead of rehabs. Less red tape, no problems with shaky *foundations*, *leaks,* or other problems that you tend to run across when you're trying to *flip* something *old,*" Chase served up another rebuttal.

Kassidy and her mother's heads bounced back and forth as they quietly observed the match of wits playing out before them. While Kassidy assumed that her father was just grilling Chase in a routine assertion of authority, Maria wearily read the hidden connotations behind their words. She was well aware of the inner workings of Kameron's new position with the HIDTA, and as she caught the true meaning of Kameron's jabs, she became mildly worried about how Chase figured into Kameron's dealings.

"So a nice little *small time* real estate pop up...what's the name of your firm?"

"Dad! Really? That's so rude of you!" Kassidy snapped.

"How the hell am I rude asking questions in *my* house where *I* pay the mortgage with *honest* money?"

"Kameron, that's enough!" Maria chimed in, visibly irritated with her husband's snide insinuations. "Chase is a guest in our home, please don't be so crass."

Having now picked up on the tension between the adults, Kassidy's siblings looked on in awe at the heated scene that played out before them, unsure of whether to be intrigued by the drama or rattled by their father's brooding mood.

"It's enough when I say it's enough," Kameron snapped, turning his attention to Kassidy. "Kass, if this is *all* you want in a boyfriend, you don't want much."

"Okay, now that's my cue to leave. I'm not about to sit here and listen–" Kassidy began before Chase chimed in.

"It's okay beautiful, no sweat. Trust, it takes more than a few verbal jabs to get under my skin. It's all good," Chase said before turning to Maria. "Mrs. Kingston, this was a lovely meal that you prepared, and I appreciate the invite." Chase turned to Kameron to speak next. "Mr. Kingston, lovely home that you have; looks like *your* mortgage dollars are put to good use," Chase retorted, rising to his feet and leaning down to kiss Kassidy's forehead.

"Wait Chase! You don't have to leave, darling. I'm sure my husband was–"

"Oh he can leave. He can DEFINITELY leave–right out the same door he came in," Kameron interrupted, dropping his napkin on his plate as he stood up.

"I can't believe you Dad!" Kassidy sassed. Chase turned to leave, stopping at Maria's seat just as she rose to her feet.

"I'm terribly sorry about all of this Chase, please don't think this is how we usually treat our guests," Maria sighed.

"No apology needed, Mrs. Kingston. Thanks again," Chase assured before turning to Kassidy. He gave her a knowing glance that spoke volumes. He didn't want his presence to further aggravate the evening but mostly, Chase didn't want Kassidy on the receiving end of Kameron's tirade when he knew that he was the true cause of Kameron's animosity. Chase's eyes pled with Kassidy to leave with

him, and hers replied that she had to speak her piece to her father before leaving–minus his presence.

"Kass, give me a call when you're on your way home. I need to know that you're okay," Chase affirmed; she winked her appreciation for his concern.

"Let me see you out, sweetheart," Maria offered, seizing the opportunity to smooth over Kameron's rude behavior.

"Thanks, I appreciate that," Chase smiled. *Such a sweetheart; like mother like daughter,* Chase thought to himself.

Fastening his seatbelt as he backed out of the driveway, Chase chuckled to himself as he thought about how he could nearly see the steam rising from Kameron's head.

"Pops was heated," Chase laughed out loud. "It's all good though. A few grandbabies will calm that fool right on down."

Caught by a stoplight, he decided to shoot Kassidy a quick text since he had every intention of seeing her later; he had plans to make sure her night ended on a good note, in spite of her bitch ass daddy's temper tantrum.

CHASE: *Hit me when u get 2 da crib. I'm comin thru*

When Kassidy didn't respond right away, he figured that she was still talking her way out of her parents' house, so he decided to swing through and check on a few of his spots before heading to her side of town. As he rode, he mulled over how small the Island really was, and how there was some truth to the theory of six degrees of separation. Never in a million years would he have imagined himself standing in the dining room of Special Agent Kameron Kingston.

Back at Kassidy's parents' house, Kameron had retreated to the back deck to calm his nerves. Downing the last gulp of his Hennessey Black, he dug his cell phone out of his pocket to interrupt dinner for one of the agents he worked with. *Shit, my evening's ruined; might as well piss on his parade too,* Kameron thought. The other agent answered on the third ring.

"Yeah, what's up?"

"Guess who the fuck I just put out my damn house?"

"Your side chick," the agent joked.

"Fuckin' Baptiste!" Kameron boomed.

"Get the fuck outta here!"

"Shit just got real..." Kameron affirmed.

Chapter 12

KASSIDY: *On my way now*

Kassidy smiled at Chase's text; it was just what she needed after escaping yet another *Kameron Kingston Krackdown.* She loved her father to the moon and back, but the stunt he pulled that night was one for the record books. While she didn't expect him to welcome Chase with open arms, she certainly didn't think he'd show his ass the way he did. In spite of the disaster that dinner turned out to be, she was pleased that her mother seemed to take to Chase, and he was the perfect gentleman the entire evening. Kassidy was impressed with the way that Chase stood his ground and didn't let her father punk him; most guys would have either snapped with some sort of disrespectful response, or completely backed down. Chase affirmed yet again that he was indeed a boss, and Kassidy found herself even more turned on than before.

Just as she made it inside her home and kicked her shoes off, her doorbell was ringing. Knowing it was Chase, she perked up immediately and hoped that he wasn't completely turned off by her father's overbearing display of theatrics at dinner.

"Babe, you came," Kassidy smiled, burying her face in his chest.

"Of course *ya man* came. You know I got you," Chase whispered in her ear, swallowing her trim physique in a big bear hug. "You good, ma?"

"Yeah I'm fine… I'm used to my dad's craziness, believe me. Are you okay though? He was rude as hell–I'm so sorry."

"First of all, don't you ever apologize for the actions of another man–ever. Second of all, ain't no real man gonna be thrown by the words of another man. Believe me, your father ain't the first nigga to wanna knock Baptiste, and he won't be the last. I ain't even mad to tell you the truth. Shit, a nigga is supposed to go hard for his

baby girl; that's what dads do. Besides, ain't nothing or no one keepin' me from *my woman*."

"You mean you don't think my family is completely insane?" Kassidy leaned her head back, resting her chin on Chase's chest as she got lost in his chestnut-brown eyes.

"Ma, I ain't got nothin' but love for my in-laws," he joked.

"You so silly boy, get in there," Kassidy playfully pushed Chase through the doorway, closing it and securing the locked behind them.

"But for real though, thanks for coming to dinner. You're a brave dude standing up to Kameron Kingston."

"Anything for you, ma," Chase whispered, lifting her chin with his index fingers.

Their gazes locked for what seemed like an eternity, both reading each other's desire without a single spoken word. Kassidy saw a guy that was worlds away from the thug that the streets knew; she saw a Goliath-like warrior, willing to face nearly any obstacle for her. In Kassidy, Chase saw a girl far from the streets, miles away from what had become a way of life for him. She was just what he needed; a thriving rose reaching for the sun in concrete jungle.

"What's that for?" Chase quizzed.

"What?"

"That...that smile. Like you feelin' right at home in a nigga's arms and shit."

"Boy hush...nothing, I was just thinking..."

"About what, this?" Chase asked as he leaned into Kassidy's face and pressed their lips together. He suckled her bottom lip for a second before thrusting his tongue forward, hungrily searching her mint-flavored mouth for its partner.

"Mmmm," Kassidy moaned as Chase pulled her close into his body, his right hand cradling her face as his left cupped the firmness that was her behind. Breaking their kiss, he took a step back, creating a decent space to allow him to take a full assessment of her gorgeous body. Kassidy reached for his shirt, and he rested his

arms on her shoulders as she slowly released each button before sliding the shirt down and off his arms. She looked him up and down, and her eyes seemingly fixated on the crotch of his pants.

Damn this nigga cut; he must live in the gym. Fuck...I ain't know he had it like this underneath those baggy ass clothes.

Chase interrupted Kassidy's lustful reflection of him and pulled her into another kiss, reaching down to throw her legs over his forearm as he carried her to her bedroom. Approaching the bed, Chase swung her legs around and spread them to straddle his body, then eased down onto the bed. Kassidy slid closer into him, bringing her throbbing clit to rest right on top of the stiffness that was building just beyond the zipper of his pants; Chase welcomed her with a yearning desire to dickmatize her. She captivated him with her smile as he gazed deeply into her feline eyes, and he found himself easily lost in her beauty.

Kassidy slid back off his lap and grabbed his hands, pulling him to his feet. Once he was standing, she took two steps forward to unfasten his belt. She then unbuttoned his pants and slid them down, along with his black Armani boxer briefs. Chase stepped out of his clothing, letting it fall to the floor. Needing her flesh next to his ASAP, Chase slid his hands down the back of her romper and slid it down. Her braless C cups sprung free, nipples standing pert in salute of the fine specimen of man that stood before them.

Kassidy's clothing joined Chase's on the floor, leaving her in a cherry blossom T-Back thong. Chase looped a finger around each of the side straps and with a powerful jerk, sent them flying to the floor. Returning to his seated position on the bed, Chase pulled Kassidy into his lap once again, relishing the absence of the clothing barrier, her wetness now skin-to-skin with the stiffness of his erection. Kassidy whispered his name as he embraced her around her tiny waist, her mouth falling from grace as he slid his mass inside of her.

"Ahhhhh..." Kassidy groaned as she took in every inch of his lengthy dick, her breath catching briefly in her chest as she adjusted to his size.

Long strokes and deep breaths echoed throughout the room, as Kassidy straddled Chase's dick and gave him a ride to remember. She was in full control, and was aiming to please her bad boy. The bed screeched, juices leaked, and intense moans escaped their mouths. Tender kisses were harmonized with deep pounds while their heartbeats synchronized in rhythm, as if they were one. Their bodies grinded up against one another as perspiration misted their skin. Kassidy was in a zone, transported to a vulnerable state of ecstasy as her body surrendered to the will of Chase's dick.

"Oh yes...fuck me bae, fuck me," crept through her lips as his tongue outlined every inch of her sensuous silhouette.

Chase slowly lapped at the ebb and flow of her perspiration as it meandered down to her belly. He taunted her nipples with playful nibbles, assaulting her breasts with a frenzied tongue-lashing of circular stimulation. Chase then cupped each breast and force-fed himself as if his life depended on it. He buried his face in Kassidy's chest as her fingers tightly gripped a handful of his freshly twisted locks, forcing his head to briefly retreat from the soft comfort of her breasts.

"Look at me," Kassidy whispered as she stared into Chase's fiery eyes, which burned with desire. She wanted him to witness her fuck faces firsthand; her inner goddess knew that this was a show he wouldn't soon forget.

Chase swiftly flipped Kassidy onto her back, sliding his dick right back up into the deep wetness of her love folds; this time, he was in full control, intent on asserting his position as *her man.* Chase packed her pussy with his entire shaft as moans eluded her pursed lips. Kassidy's eyebrows furrowed up as her face began to tense up— not because she wasn't enjoying him, but because his ego was bigger than she expected. Chase pushed in deeper, until she pleaded with him to stop.

"Take it," Chase uttered as he continued to stroke her.

Kassidy braced herself so she'd be able to sustain him beating up the pussy. She was finally able to relax a bit as she closed her eyes.

"Open your eyes and look at me," he demanded as he looked deeply into Kassidy's cat-like eyes, sliding her legs up over his shoulders just enough to dig all the way in; he enjoyed the view of her sex faces from his front row seat. "This my pussy now," Chase continued as his rhythm grew faster.

"Mmmm…ssss…yours…mmmm…shit," Kassidy moaned her agreement.

Between Kassidy's wetness and Chase ramming his dick inside of her, her walls starting making sounds as a little air seeped in.

"That's right, talk to daddi. Ohhhh...this some good fucking pussy," Chase moaned as he continued his piercing stare into Kassidy's eyes.

"Give it to me, daddi. Yessss yesss, give it to me. Fuck!"

Chase took his shaft out but he kept Kassidy's legs on his shoulders, pulling her cheeks up to his face as she continued to lay on her back. Her ass was in the air, and Chase's face was buried in her deep ocean of lust. He made soft, wet, circular motions around her lips as he sucked, pulled, and teased her clit. Her clit was the surfboard, riding the wave that was his tongue. Chase's mouth was the perfect storm, and Kassidy's pussy loved catching the wave. She paddled hard with her hips as she glided with his motions. Her body was floating in the air as she desperately tried to prolong her orgasm.

"Damn, ohhhh, ahhhh, hell yeah," Kassidy muffled in pure ecstasy.

Chase continued to lick her soft place as his eyes stole a view of her face. *Imma make you mine,* he thought to himself as he watched her squirm. Kassidy slowly dropped her body back to the bed and held Chase's head up as she tried to distract her thoughts,

fighting so she wouldn't nut so quickly. She sat up and leaned her body forward as she pushed him back onto the bed. She placed her hand around his shaft and massaged it with her hand before leaning forward and to slide him into her mouth; using her A-1 suction lock, she delivered a passionate assault as she continued to glide her hand up and down his pole.

"Damn," Chase moaned as Kassidy's mouth exerted control of his hard piece.

Her saliva drizzled out a lustful lubrication onto his mouthful of missile, as she alternated her sucking with the grinding massage of her hands. She bobbed her head up and down as the tip of his dick tickled her tonsils, her gag reflex nonexistent.

Feeling his center slipping away, Chase cupped Kassidy's face, his fingers lightly caressing the back of her earlobes. As the speed of Kassidy's bobbing increased, Chase's fingers became entangled in her mess of curls; he gripped a handful of her hair, restricting her range of motion as he felt his climax approaching.

Chase feverishly pumped into Kassidy's face, the arch of his back now causing his hips to bounce off the bed. Kassidy further relaxed her throat to accommodate his momentum as her saliva sloppily coated his veiny flesh; she dipped her hand underneath his sack and teased his balls in a juggling motion, sending Chase over the top.

"Ahhhh fuuuuuck, shiiiiiit!" Chase growled and pumped vigorously as his orgasm shot out full-force down Kassidy's esophagus. She relaxed her jaws to accommodate the overflow of his semen while tightening the lock of her suction, refusing to spill even a drop of his love. As Chase's pumping slowed to a halt, Kassidy finished her meal, greedily sucking the last bit of cum from his head before planting a deep, sensual kiss right on his tip.

"Ahh, hol' up ma," Chase winced, his body still sensitive from the rush of ecstasy that still danced across the nerve endings of his dick.

Kassidy laid her head on Chase's washboard stomach as he collected himself. She placed a soft kiss on his six-pack, and another on his thigh. He softly stroked the top of her head as he closed his eyes for a split second. *Damn...shorty head game right...fuck they mean pretty women don't give good head.* He laughed to himself, feeling humored by his thoughts; feeling the movement in his abdomen, Kassidy raised her head up.

"What's funny bae?"

"Ah...nothing, beautiful. Just tripping off some shit that nigga Lando said."

"So you're here with me and you're thinking about Lando?" Kassidy teasingly pouted.

"Nah... not really. Something he said earlier just popped in my head, but that was it. Shiiii, my thoughts are on you and how I need you to be my baby."

"Your baby? What do you mean?"

"You know what I mean. Me as your man...you as my girl."

"Nah, why you get to be the man and I get to be the girl? Why can't I be your woman?"

Chase lightly laughed. "You know what I mean ma, same difference."

"Yeah, I know what you mean. So you were serious about that *I'm your man* thing, huh?"

"No doubt. I thought you knew. I mean everything I say. I don't make empty promises."

"Hmm…is that right?"

"What you mean hmm…damn right it's right."

"Nothing really, I just said hmm..."

"But you didn't answer my question."

Kassidy crawled up to the top of the bed. She laid on her side, facing him as he laid on his back, head turned and eyes locked with hers.

"Technically, you didn't ask me to be your girl, you told me you need me to be your baby. Yes, Chase, I would love to be your girl. Your woman, that is."

"You better."

Kassidy leaned in and gave him a soft peck, then rested her head on his chest, smiling at the rhythmic drumming of his heartbeat. *Her man's heartbeat.* Chase pulled her closer into his body, running his hand up and down her thighs before resting it on the curve of her ass. Feeling complete, he drifted off to sleep with his baby in his arms. *His baby.*

Chapter 13

3 Months Later

"Mmmmm damn ma, you gon' make me miss my flight fuckin' around with these damn lips," Chase breathed on Kassidy's lips as he planted what was seemingly an endless flurry of kisses; she exhaled a breathy moan as he caught the outer rim of her bottom lip between his teeth.

"Mmm...I got something you can nibble on," Kassidy cooed.

"Nah for real tho bae, I gotta run, you know that nigga Lando drive reckless as hell when he rushin'," Chase countered, planting a final kiss on Kassidy's lips, followed by one on her forehead.

"Call me when you land?"

"You already know...and keep ya hands out my shit while I'm gone."

"Really bae? For two whole days?" Kassidy whined, sliding her hands down into her boy shorts and parting her honey folds with her index finger.

"What I say?" Chase scoffed, leaning over to remove her hands from her shorts. He plunged her fingers into his mouth, greedily sucking them clean of her juices that tasted like she had eaten some pineapples.

"Mmmm, shit ma! Lemme stop fuckin' around and go, for real this time. Aight bae, I'm out," Chase fell into one last kiss before breaking away and heading downstairs.

"Bae!" Kassidy yelled.

"Yeah ma, what's up?"

"I love you!" she shouted, waiting to see if he'd finally return the sentiment.

"I got you ma," Chase smiled. Kassidy wasn't entirely bothered that he didn't say it back. They'd discussed the "L" word before, so she knew it was a tender subject for him, but she swore

with everything in her that he felt it–even if he couldn't say it. *Look at me now, in love with a hitta,* Kassidy thought to herself as she flopped back down on the bed, curling herself into Chase's pillow and drowning in his scent.

*** *** ***

Chase and Lando had just landed in St. Louis and after grabbing their ride, they headed to meet up with their new team. Chase was put on to the new setup out in St. Louis by Mark, who came up on the block with him back in the day. They met while playing together on the basketball team at the Boys & Girls Club, and rocked hard with each other until Mark's mom relocated to St. Louis for work. Even though they had lost touch the past few years, Mark still held Chase down and brought business to the table from time to time, so when he called and kicked it to Chase that St. Louis was dry, it was an offer Chase couldn't refuse.

"So when we 'spose to get up with that nigga Mark?" Lando inquired.

"Should touch down tonight. Told him to hit me up."

"You sure these new soldiers straight?" Lando pressed.

Chase had top-notch instincts, like he was CIA or something, and even though Lando trusted Chase's decision to make things jump off in the Midwest, he wasn't too sure about the way that nigga Mark moved.

"Nigga, you the boss now? The fuck I look like puttin' some fraud ass niggas down?"

"Chill nigga, I'm just makin' sure thangs sun. You be lockin' in on them stacks and shit sometimes."

"Nigga if you ain't sure then fall back," Chase snapped, growing irritated with Lando's second-guessing. "This my shit, Imma move how the fuck I see fit, ya dig?"

"Aight man," Lando sighed, shaking his head and shifting his gaze out the window at the passing scenery. He'd mute his concerns for the time being, but he still planned to watch how that nigga Mark moved.

About an hour later, they were pulling up at what would serve as the main spot for Chase's operation out that way. Chase had been back and forth scouting spots out the past few weeks, and he had his boy Cybo lay it out with all the high tech shit that made him sleep well at night; Cybo was going to be Chase's right hand for the operation out in the 'Lou. Pulling the truck close to the back door, Chase and Lando exited and made their way into the building, down the back hallway, and into the main warehouse area.

"What's good C, what up niggas?" Chase dapped Cybo, then went down the line and gave the rest of his team pounds. He had a total of six cats on the team, all hungry and ready to get paid.

"What y'all got for me?" Chase began, hands tucked in his pockets.

"E'rythang up and running. First shipment be here tomorrow. I figure we check it, break it down, and push it out. E'rybody know what they gotta do."

"Aight, drops?" Chase turned to Cybo, seeing if he'd followed his recommendations.

"Slim," Cybo replied, nodding in Slim's direction.

"Bens?" Chase continued.

"All me, nobody touches the money but me," Cybo shot back.

"Aight. What the numbers lookin' like?" Chase probed.

"Test run was clutch. Spots dried up by second day; damn fiends was like Walkin' Dead and shit...shit def gonna blow," Cybo detailed.

"Aight, so for now, product should come in every two weeks, so keep that shit movin'. Y'all get that shit on warp, we'll up the bricks. Product's there, and it's stacks to be made, so y'all niggas show me what y'all got," Chase instructed, making eye contact with each of them to make sure they were all on the same page.

"No doubt," Cybo confirmed.

"What else?" Chase questioned.

"Y'all clear?" Cybo turned to the team, and all nodded confirmation except Slim. "What's the deal? Cybo prodded him.

"Ay, some nigga came through the spot lookin' for boss man this mornin', said you needed to come see him. Spanish cat, ol' Rico Suave lookin' nigga," Slim outlined.

"And you just now droppin' this shit..." Chase interrupted.

"I was–"

"Nigga, you 'bout to be a WAS if you let some shit slip off yo' plate again. You confused 'bout the chain or some shit?" Chase hissed, stepping close to Slim and looking him dead in the eye.

"Nah man–"

"Clearly you are, cuz I ain't yo' nigga."

"Nah boss man, I got it," Slim corrected himself, holding Chase's gaze even though he was nervous as shit on the inside.

"Anybody else got any fuckin' secrets up in this bitch?" Chase boomed, irritated by all their asses. Seeing everyone was on mute, Chase dismissed everyone.

"Aight. We out, get to ya spots–Cybo, tomorrow at six. Eyes up," Chase finished, letting Cybo know to sync all surveillance feeds from all properties in town to his phone.

"Fasho," Cybo dapped Chase and Lando as they headed back out to their truck.

***

The next evening, Chase, Lando, Cybo, and Slim met back up at the warehouse to accept shipment of the product. Mark joined them just before the product came through; he stayed around for a few to kick it, while Cybo and Slim broke the product down into the orders that would be delivered to each trap. Wrapping up his conversations, Mark departed a few minutes before Chase and Lando left the warehouse.

"Ay, Cybo clocked that nigga Slim said was tryin' to get at you. Down with some nigga they call Zo. Dominican cat. Name ringin' in the streets. Sound like that nigga got shop here." Lando paused and huffed before he shared the next piece of info. "Had a

bounty on Mark's head," he finished, giving Chase a side-glance to see what his reaction was.

"Aight. We touch down in Jersey tomorrow. That nigga Mark need to get at me ASAP before I'm wheels up," Chase commanded; Lando read his demand loud and clear as he read an incoming text from Cybo.

"Word. Ay, all the spots got stock, that nigga–"

BOOM!

"What the fu–" Chase shouted as they were rammed from the back; a few seconds later, gunfire rang out as their truck swerved into the guardrail.

"Shit!" Lando shouted, pulling his piece from his hip and reaching under the seat for the sawed off shotgun that was tucked away. Chase fought to correct the steering as Lando returned fire.

"Fuck!" Chase boomed, pounding his rage into the steering wheel as he put as much distance between them and the van that had rammed them. *Not even on ground for 24 hours niggas already bustin' at us?* Chase fumed to himself, beyond heated.

Emptying the clip in his Sig Sauer, Lando lit the van up with the shotgun; one strategic shot sent the van over the guardrail. Flipping several times, the van came to rest on its driver side and burst into flames a few minutes later. Chase sped up, merging from the access road onto I-170.

"Yo, what the fuck!" Lando snapped.

"Get that nigga Cybo on the line, straight the fuck up!" Chase barked.

Lando followed orders and let Cybo know to meet them in a few.

"Ay, where that nigga Mark went to?" Lando pointed a subliminal finger. "I know you ain't tryin' to hear that shit, but that nigga foul as fuck, yo. The fuck he know a nigga tight 'bout some shit in the streets and he hand you that shit with a straight face? That's some snake shit, B," Lando continued.

Chase remained silent, clenching his jaw as he mulled whether or not he was going to put Mark on his back before they flew out the next day.

Chapter 14

Since their trip to St. Louis a few weeks ago, Chase and Lando had eyes on Mark to keep close watch on how he moved. They suspected he had something to do with who the fools that shot at them, who they later learned were connected to a cat by the name of Zo. Chase was a man of calculated moves though, so he wanted to make sure he dug up as much info as he could, especially since Mark had already been less than forthcoming with details.

Meanwhile, Chase was doing everything he could to keep drama and confusion from raining on the parade of love he'd been enjoying with Kassidy. He'd let all the random chicks he'd kicked it with in the past know that he was off the market, and warned them not to even think of stepping to Kassidy with any bullshit. Chase wasn't one to put his hands on a woman, but he had a roster of goons that had no problems roughing women up, so the chicks knew better than to try him. So far, everyone was playing their role like well-behaved little girls except for Meka.

Meka made her feelings known to Chase every chance she got, and she continued to ring his phone on some hotline bling shit. She was well aware of who little Ms. Kassidy was, and she had every intention of dethroning her to claim what she believed was her rightful spot on the throne–next to Chase.

Chase had just wrapped up meeting Lando and the rest of his Staten Island crew, and was headed home to Kassidy when his phone buzzed an unwelcome interruption to what had been a pretty good day for him. Eyes on the road due to the heavy traffic, Chase answered the call using his in-dash Bluetooth without checking his caller ID.

"Yo."

"Bae, why haven't I heard from you all day?"

Fuck, Chase silently cursed, wishing he'd just let Meka roll over to voicemail. When he didn't reply, Meka had to check to make sure he was still on the line.

"Hello? You there?"

Nah bitch. "Ay, what up?"

"What you mean what up? I haven't seen you in forever, like you avoiding me or some shit...you act like you ain't got time for me no more now that you all boo'd up," Meka snapped, fuming that Chase had the nerve to go and get exclusive with some other chick when she'd been playing wifey, fucking and sucking him dry for the better part of a year.

"Chill with that, you know what it is. I already told you I ain't tryin' to go there with you no more," Chase brushed Meka off.

"So you just cut me off like that? Like I ain't shit to you? That's foul as fuck, Chase!"

"Ma, all that ain't even necessary...you mad cool, but I got a girl now. We been through this, so why you actin' brand new?"

"Nigga, we done when I say we're done. Don't even try to play me like th–"

"Ay lemme hit you back," Chase disconnected the call, interrupting Meka's tirade. He dropped his head back against his headrest, dragging his hand from his forehead down to his chin.

Meka was the kinda trouble he didn't need at that moment. With the situation out in St. Louis and the little no-name niggas that kept trying to catch them slipping on the Island, home was one of the only place Chase had peace in his life at the moment. He promised Kassidy that he would keep any and all drama concerning other chicks from ever reaching their doorstep, and that there'd never be a competition for his affection and devotion. After witnessing Meka's little verbal tantrum, Chase just hoped that was a promise he could keep.

***

Ever since being shot at after leaving the warehouse that one night, Chase was always on edge anytime they had to travel to

St. Louis. He started to second-guess his decision to take over Mark's operation, especially since it looked like the beef between Mark and Zo was some deep shit that went way back, but with the money flowing in so fast they barely had enough time to clean it, Chase was in too deep to just walk away.

Cybo had finally come through with the info Chase needed to get to the bottom of the real reason Zo seemed to be gunning for him, so he and Lando were back in town to handle Mark so they could focus on handling that nigga Zo.

"That nigga Cybo got him primed and waitin'," Lando relayed the content of Cybo's text as Chase flew down I-170, heading to The Knock–the spot where they laid snitches and enemies to rest.

"Aight...tell him that nigga Mark is mine. Imma lay that nigga down myself," Chase ordered.

An hour later, they pulled up to the spot and headed inside. Chase planned to get the shit over with quick and be balls deep in Kassidy's pussy before midnight. Heading to one of the back rooms, they found Mark unconscious and gagged, his wrists and ankles bound as he dangled from a meat hook that was secured to a retractable ceiling track.

"So, this nigga made a deal with the devil when he got in bed with Zo...jacked him for his own shit, then tried to turn around and sell that shit right under Zo's nose, on blocks he knew this nigga ran. Zo gave him a small quad of the hood, let this nigga eat and shit, and he got greedy. When he got word on the hit on his head, he hit you up; figured he'd let you slide in and take over operations, and shift the target to your back," Cybo ran down all the details he'd gathered in the past week.

Chase paced the floor back and forth, hands tucked in his pockets as he willed himself to calm down. He could count on two fingers the number of times he'd been played in his entire life, the current situation being one. He was only mildly irritated at being played; what he was more upset about was that the betrayal came

from someone he considered to be his boy, someone he went way back with–someone that *knew* he wasn't to be fucked with.

Cybo passed a tiny wireless remote to Chase, who engaged the power switch and waited a minute or so before the charge indicator light shined a bright green *ready* signal. Chase used the small keypad to set the electric current to 30 milliamps, then pressed enter. A second later, Mark's body sprang to life as he trembled and jerked against the surge of electricity dancing through his body.

"My mannnnn Mark…what's good nigga?" Chase taunted as Mark's eyes bulged with terror.

"All this time you've known a nigga…all those bodies you caught with me…at what point did a nigga's name become Madden?" Chase added; Mark continued to wriggle against the restraints that immobilized his extremities. Just as his body relaxed, Chase punched 75 into the keypad and pressed enter, sending a second surge through Mark's body–this one robbing Mark of bladder and bowel control.

"You know I'd normally blast a nigga twice and keep it movin', right?" Chase continued. "Lucky for you, a nigga feelin' generous today." Mark's face contorted into a confused frown.

"A nigga's trigger finger is on chill today, so you get a pass," Chase began, "You cold?" Chase quipped, observing the shivers that now consumed Mark's body. "Bruh, I ain't heartless, so lemme help you warm up," and with a final entry of 150 on the keypad, Chase sent one last stream of electricity into Mark's body. He leaned against the wall, crossing his arms as he brought a foot to rest flat against the wall. A minute ticked by as the whites of Mark's eyes replaced his dilated pupils. Another minute passed before smoke billowed from Mark's flesh, his body smoldering from the inside out. Chase waited for the involuntary spasms to cease before he spoke.

"Get them niggas out here to clean this shit up," Chase ordered, tossing Cybo a demanding glance. "We out Lando, gotta get home and fuck my girl."

Chapter 15

Kassidy and Mia were at Chase's condo, which looked more like a mansion. She'd been living with Chase for the past few months; after spending nearly every night there and taking over the closet in one of his guest rooms, Chase suggested that she officially move in. He knew he'd rest better at night with *his woman* under his roof. Kassidy kept her house that her father gifted her when she went off to college, but had moved all of her personal belongings into Chase's place. As much as she knew Chase was the one for her, she refused to be drunk in love and wind up with nothing of her own in the end.

So far, Kassidy and Chase's relationship was in a good place. He had left all the jumps offs alone, and focused more on his money and his love with Kassidy; not that pussy ever flustered Chase's thoughts about stacking his paper anyway.

Kassidy was happy; she never thought that a street dude like Chase would be the man of her dreams, and she was very so much dangerously in love. Nobody could tell her nothing about Chase, not even her girl Mia. Kassidy was definitely gone in the head, and whoever had beef with Chase had beef with her–that was her mindset. Kassidy had buckled down and finally decided to take some online classes. She also held down a part-time job as a Clinical Psychology Assistant at HIDTA, where her father Kameron worked. Chase told her that she really didn't need to work, although he supported her taking online classes so she could finally finish school. He loved spending quality time with his girl; nothing like the hit and run arrangement that he had with other chicks in the past. From trips around the world to fancy dinners and movie nights curled up on the couch, every minute spent with Chase made Kassidy feel complete.

Daddy Kingston had backed off a bit once he found out Kassidy was taking classes again, but he didn't know that his precious KK had moved in with her boyfriend; the street hustling

thug that he despised and couldn't wait to bring down–him and his entire organization. *Another fight at another time,* Kameron Kingston believed, but soon enough he would bear witness to the fall of one of the Island's most notorious drug lords–so he thought anyway.

***

Kassidy and Mia caught up on girl talk as they sipped on some wine and watched a little television; at least, the television watched them.

"Bitch, I told you that you were going to turn into the old cat lady. Look at your ass all boo'd up and shit, and I don't even see your ass as much as I used to," Mia said as she passed the swisher, fat with mango kush.

"Girl, I know right? I'm just really trying to focus on school right now. Ain't nothing out there anyway. I got my man," Kassidy teased as she took a few puffs of the fruity kush and passed it back to Mia. Kassidy was more of a social smoker, so she rarely indulged unless Mia came around.

"Where yo' nigga at now? You know them hoes always be comin' at him. Why you stay posted up in the house? You don't even be watchin' yo' nigga?"

"Mia, if I have to watch him like a hawk, we don't need to be together. Chase loves me and I trust him."

"Yeah okay. That's the same thing ole girl said until she found my number in her man's phone and called me up talking 'bout... '*You know Trey?*' I was like bitch if you don't miss me with the bullshit and get off the other end of my line."

"I see your ass is still with the *leave the money on the nightstand* shit, huh?"

"And you know this boo," Mia winked as the mango-infused smoke flooded her lungs.

"So girl...are you back to talking to your parents yet? I mean, don't you think it's time to move forward and let the past be the

past? Shit, all families have secrets; just let it go and forgive them for lying to you?"

"Fuck no! Once I find out what I need to find out, then we can work on moving forward. I hired a PI to look into it for me and I should be hearing something soon."

"I feel you boo, if it were me I'm sure I'd do the same thing too. Yo, you know what I've been meaning to tell you?"

"What?" Mia asked as she reached for the ashtray, putting the thoughts of her parents into the back of her mind.

"You know Chase's homeboy Lando, right?"

"Yassss bitch, of course I know his fine ass."

Kassidy chuckled at her friend's dramatics. "Well check this out. Every time I see that nigga, he's always asking where you at on the sly."

"Bitch you lying?" Mia said as she stood up in the middle of the floor.

"Calm down trick. And yes, anytime he sees me and you ain't with me, he be on some Dora shit, trying to see if you coming in behind me or some shit. I think he's feelin' you."

"And why are you just telling me this! Biiiitch...you know I got a little crush on Lando's FINE ass."

Kassidy burst into laughter at Mia's enthusiasm. "I know, I know, I know...it kinda just slipped my mind. You know when I'm not gone with Chase somewhere my ass be in here up in these books."

"Girl, where he at now? You got that nigga number? Call Chase and get it–" Mia anxiously rambled before Kassidy cut her off.

"Calm down, thirsty. Wait...I just got an idea."

"What bitch what?! Stop withholding information from a bitch."

"Mia! Calm your ass down and listen," Kassidy continued to laugh. Mia took a seat Indian-style on the floor, as if she was a kindergartner at story time.

"Well...Chase invited me to Lando's grand opening tonight; you know he got a new sports bar. I told him I had to study and I couldn't go with him, but now that you're here and we haven't hung in a minute...do you want to–" but before Kassidy could finish her sentence, Mia cut her off.

"Yasss bitch, yasss...let's go."

Kassidy continued to laugh as the effects of the wine and the kush started to kick in. She hadn't chilled with her bestie Mia in a minute, and she didn't want the night to end. After a few more laughs, they both got dolled up and headed out to the grand opening of Lando's new spot, Premier Lounge.

Chapter 16

"Girl, this is nice! Lando doing it big I see. Hmmm, where his fine ass at?"

"They over there, you don't see 'em?"

"Oh yeah, I see 'em. Look at your man though. As soon as he saw it was you, his face lit up like a damn Christmas tree. You two are starting to get on my last damn nerve, I swear," Mia joked.

"Girllll, love will do that to you. Look at my baby. Damn...every time I see him it's like the first time all over again," Kassidy said as she smiled and kept her eyes on Chase.

"Ughhh...enough already! Come introduce me," Mia said as she pulled Kassidy by the arm and walked her over to Chase, Lando, and the crew.

"Hey ma, you came," Chase said as he stood up and hugged Kassidy.

"Yeah, Mia stopped over and I thought it would be a good idea to take a study break for a minute, and come chill with my baby and the fellas."

"Oh, so Mia can get you out but your man can't?" Chased teased as he hugged her and placed a soft kiss onto her lips.

"Ahhh...you know it ain't even like that babe. It's just..."

Before she could finish her sentence. Mia interrupted her by clearing her throat as a signal for Kassidy to reintroduce her to Lando, who sat there eyeing Mia's ass as if it was wild animal kingdom and her ass was the prey.

"Heyyyyyy Chase," Mia playfully cooed.

"What's good ma?" Chase said as he thought for a minute that if it had not been for Mia bringing Kassidy to the park that day, they probably wouldn't be a couple. "Good seeing you again. It's been a minute."

"Wayyy too long. I guess after you and my girl hooked up, there was no need for me..."

Kassidy cleared her throat. "Lando...Lando...um...this is Mia. You know Miaaaa..." she said as she smiled, eyes widened; Lando gave her an easy smile in return.

"No doubt, of course, Mia. What's up love?" Lando said as he stood up and walked over to Mia, Chase, and Kassidy, and extended his hand out to her.

"You got it daddi. What's up with you?" Mia asked as she smiled.

"You love. I've been trying to see what's up with you but I'm glad you came through tonight."

"Fa sho. I'm glad I came too," Mia smiled.

"Mia, come with me to the restroom for a second."

"Right nowwww?" Mia mumbled through her teeth as she steadily smiled at Lando, calculating a ballpark figure of his money in her head as she estimated what it must cost to open a sports bar like the one they stood in; it had wall to wall high-definition flat screens and furnishings that looked like they belonged in an upscale sports lounge. Not to mention, he was Chase's right hand man.

"Yes chiiiiiiick–right now," Kassidy teased through her tight lips. "Bae, going to powder my nose, I'll be right back," she told Chase.

"Aight, I'll be here beautiful."

Kassidy gave him a peck on his lips and grabbed Mia's hand, then walked towards the restroom.

"Don't you move, daddi. I will definitely be right back," Mia flirted as she turned around and gave Lando a bedroom glance. Lando winked at her, eyes trained on her ass while she switched off toward the back of the building.

"Bring your hot ass on," Kassidy said as they came within a few feet of the restroom.

"What bitch, whatttt? What are you doing? I was just about to slide up in my spot next to Lando."

"Yeah I know, and I know you–that's why I needed to talk to you first," Kassidy demanded as they walked into the restroom,

which was crowded with three other women. Two of them occupied two of the four stalls while pissing out their liquor, and the last one waited for her friends to come out as she fixed her makeup in the mirror. Kassidy walked Mia to the end of the restroom.

"What is it Kass, why you trippin'? What was so important that you had to drag me allll the way into the damn restroom right when–"

"Mia...don't take this the wrong way boo...but I just wanna run something by you right quick. Listen...I know you wanna get with Lando and all, but how 'bout you do something different with him? Save something for later; don't jump into bed with him right away–especially not tonight."

Mia gave Kassidy a weird gaze. She was trying to figure out where she was coming from, and why all of a sudden she wanted to warn her about Lando.

"What are you talking about, Kass? You know how I get down. Ain't no shame in my game. I wants my check from any nigga who's taking up my time, and I don't have a problem putting it out there from the get go."

"I know Mia, but I think he's really into you. Like I said, he's ALWAYS asking about you. If you play your cards right, you can get way more out of Lando than just some money left on the nightstand. Ya feel me?"

Mia smiled. "Yeah boo, I feel you. Good looking out. College girl makes a lot of sense and I can't even lie, I'm kinda feelin' him too–beyond his pockets. I guess I can hold out...make him wait to taste the cake."

"Right, I'm tellin' you, you wanna just win a game or the championship?"

"What, you a damn commentator now and shit?" Mia joked.

"Whatever bitch–anyway, that's all I wanted to say, had to catch your ass before you tricked the man up in yo' bed by the end of the night," Kassidy winked.

"Bitch how you knew?"

"You're my home girl, of course I know you. Just so you know...I didn't sleep with Chase until months later–believe it or not. Not that I ain't want him tearin' it up cuz dammmmm. But nah, I needed to know that I wasn't gonna be just another one of his jump offs, and look at us now. *All eyes on us*," Kassidy explained.

"And them grimy ass hoes out there definitely got they eyes on yo' man. You see them out there? How they all eye fuckin' him and shit?" Mia frowned at her friend.

"Girl, that is my least worry, trust me. I got that."

"I know that's right and... you got a point about Lando. But damnnnn...I didn't know a nigga like Chase would wait that long for the pussy. Shit, I know he get it thrown at him on the reg."

"Hmm...well now you know and it wasn't *this* pussy that was getting thrown at him, and that's why he wanted it even more," Kassidy said as her lips curved up in a sassy smirk.

Mia gave her a high five, and they both began to laugh. The female who was waiting on her friends to come out of the stalls ear-hustled their entire conversation. As soon as her girls came out, she told them what she had overheard. Kassidy and Mia both walked towards the mirror to check themselves before exiting the restroom.

"Um, which one of you bitches fucking Chase?" one of the girls asked as she stood with one hand her hip.

Chapter 17

Caught off guard by the no-name chick's question, Mia looked at Kassidy, who finished touching up her makeup and then slid her lip gloss back into her clutch. *What the fuck?* She turned around from the mirror and stared the chick who asked the question dead in the eyes.

"That bitch would be me. And how is that your business?"

The chick clucked her tongue, then turned and gave her friends a knowing look. "No she ain't tryin' to get cute on a bitch," she laughed to her friends. "Aight boo boo kitty, I see you think you got a lil spot on his dick or whatever, but that's me all day, so you can fall the fuck back. Chase belongs to me, and he knows where home is."

"Hmm…yours huh?" Kassidy frowned, her face wearing a sarcastic smile. "That's funny, 'cause the last time I checked, that's my pussy he still tasting in his mouth–'kay bitch?" Kassidy clapped back, unaware that the chick laying claim to Chase was none other than Meka, his *Friday* chick.

Meka crossed the floor, closing the distance between her and Kassidy. Sensing some shit was about to pop off, Mia wedged herself between the two women; Kassidy was far from a fighter, so Mia had no intentions on letting the off-brand chick run up on her friend.

"If you plan on leaving with all ya teeth then you might wanna back up before I knock them bitches down ya throat," Mia demanded.

"And who the fuck are you?" one of the other girls stepped in.

"Chill girl, this hoe ain't talkin' bout shit," Meka calmed her friend. "Boo, ain't nobody scared of you, with ya trick or treat pussy ass; hand that shit out like it's fuckin' candy. Bye girl," Meka

rebutted to Mia, who stepped closer into her face. Meka's mini entourage stepped forward to stand side by side with their friend.

"And I damn sure hope you don't think nobody scared of yo' ass up in here...come on Kass, lemme get you back to your man...gotta make sure Lando know he got some fuckin' trash runnin' loose up in his spot," Mia chuckled as her and Kassidy stepped around the girls, snatched the restroom door open and made their way back to the VIP area.

"Next time you call yourself checking somebody 'bout *their* man, you should definitely get yo facts straight–kay bitch?" Kassidy said as they continued out of the restroom.

"That hoe need to worry 'bout how to get her stacks up, with that cheap ass dress that look like it came from City Trends and them ran over Payless shoes," Mia called over her shoulder just as the door closed behind them, sending her and Kassidy into a fit of laughter.

***

Chase and Lando dapped up a few of their boys they knew from the block out in the Stapleton housing project. While their mamas raised Chase and Lando, Stapleton made men out of them. Finally reaching Lando's office, Chase took a seat behind his desk. Chase closed the door before plopping down onto the couch, then locked his fingers together behind his head.

"Hell of a turnout, son," Chase stated.

"Hell yeah...told you this shit was gon' pop," Lando smiled as he thumbed through a stack of papers in his inbox. "'Preciate you bein' down with me too B, that's love."

"No doubt, I got you my nigga. About that though, remember I need that shit to stay on the low. You know them boyz stay tryin' to trip a nigga up," Chase instructed.

"Say no more. You mute up in this muhfucka as far as I'm concerned," Lando agreed. "But ay, what's up with KK's girl Mia?"

"Man, you already know what it is. She a bird, I don't even know why you entertain' her, you know how she gets down. You

wildin' for real B, like you ain't got a wife at home and shit," Chase chastised.

"Come on son, ain't like it's no love connection shit. I'm just tryin' to kick it with shorty for a few. Get some A-1 dome, that's 'bout it."

"Aight, I ain't a PO or no shit, so do you; just watch ya back…that hoe be on some *get money* shit."

"You already know," Lando agreed as they both rose to leave the office, heading back to their spot in VIP.

*****

Just as Chase and Lando arrived at the staircase that led up to their VIP suite, Kassidy and Mia were returning from the restroom; to Chase's dismay, Meka and her girls were hot on their heels. *Shit,* he cursed to himself, recognizing that he needed to shut Meka down before she got started. Little did he know, she already went at Kassidy in the restroom. Chase was not about to have Meka clowning at Lando's grand opening, nor would he allow her to bring any drama to Kassidy.

"There you are ma, I was about to send out an APB on y'all," Chase joked, leaning down to kiss Kassidy on her cheek; she smiled and tucked herself under his arm. Mia seized the opportunity to lay out her intentions to Lando and did the same; her heart fluttered when he willingly pulled her in close to his body. *This shit gonna be a lot easier than I thought,* she thought to herself. Before Mia could open her mouth to advance her charm, Meka made her presence known.

"I see you found you a lil play thing, Chase…I don't even know why you won't quit playin' and just bring my dick home," Meka chuckled.

"How you even get up in here?" Chase questioned.

"Why? You actin' like you don't miss me or some shit…I bet your dick miss me tho," Meka smiled devilishly.

"Ay, I already ran shit down to you ma, and what my dick does or don't do ain't none of your concern. You can clown in front

of your lil' friends if you want to, but disrespect my girl again and Imma lay hands on you, real talk," Chase affirmed, tightening his grip around Kassidy's waist.

"Nigga you know how we do, one day you knee deep in this pussy, the next you claim we just friends, the next you got you some new pussy––but where do you allllways come back home to? Me nigga. It's what we do…but I'll play along with ya lil King Kong game and shit. Boo kitty, make sure you send my dick back home when you done with it–'kay bitch?" Meka smirked as she mocked Kassidy, eyes locked on Chase as she took two steps forward into his space. Kassidy was beyond fed up with Meka, and pulled away from Chase to put an end to her thirsty little stunt.

"Bitch if you don't back the fuck up, what part of he ain't checkin' for yo ass–" Kassidy began before Chase pulled her back and cut her off.

"Ma, uh uh, we don't do that–you don't acknowledge trick ass hoes, aight? Chill, I got this," Chase asserted before turning his gaze back to Meka.

"Fuck is your problem man? On the real, you need to chill with that shit. Fuck outta here–take your ass home before you get ya ass beat up in here. Try me if you want to," Chase boomed.

"Yes, because I'm 'bout two seconds off yo' ass myself, with your disrespectful lil ass," Mia chimed in as Lando tightened his grip to keep her from running up in Meka's face.

"Yeah, I'll head there eventually–you know the address," Meka winked at Chase, then rolled her eyes at Kassidy before turning to head to the other side of the room.

***

Lorenzo "Zo" Valentino and his crew sat off in the cut, watching Chase and Lando make their way back to their private booth, stopping to dap and hug a few people before reaching their destination. The grand opening of Premier Lounge had been highly anticipated, and anyone who was anyone was there in attendance; of course, a party on the Island wouldn't be a party without a throng of

thirsty chicks on the hunt for their next come up, and Lando's grand opening was no exception.

Zo's thirsty companion of the evening was none other than Meka. She worked for one of the fastest growing real estate firms in the city, and they'd met when Zo visited the bank she often consulted with. Meka was there meeting with one of her mortgage consultant buddies while Zo was there for a meeting with the branch manager. Taken aback by Zo's honey-buttered complexion, Meka had been sure to catch his eye before he left. Little did she know, Zo's visit was far from coincidence, and he'd set his sights on getting next to her when he first saw her leaving the bank a few weeks back.

"So it would seem that these two clowns are moving more weight than I originally estimated...no way they can afford this spot making small time moves," Zo observed, his words dripping with his Dominican accent.

Watching the two from afar, Zo could slightly understand why Chase was the so-called king in the streets on the Island. He had a certain arrogance about him that demanded the respect of his minions, which was apparent in the way they scurried to make way for his entrance as he climbed the stairs to the additional VIP section on the opposite side of the building. While Zo had no personal beef, his dislike of the Haitian fool was all business–it was always business with Zo, and only when you impeded that business did things turn personal. He'd given Chase a warning, and though it would appear that Chase disregarded the cautionary notice, Zo planned to give him one last opportunity to comply. It had been over a year since he had personally dropped a body on US soil, but he was more than willing to come out of retirement if need be.

"Looks that way, Tíguere," Zo's lieutenant agreed. "Change of plans?"

"No need. These American *vividores* make your job too easy, with their flashy cars and flaunting of what they think are their riches and rewards. Look–over there. How can you determine which

pariguayo is *the boss* as they say? Just look, tell me," Zo commanded.

"Es fácil, boss. You will always know the man that has the most money if you pay attention to los aviónes. What do the street thugs say, boss? *Money brings the hoes out?*" the lieutenant laughed.

"Correct. And that is why Señorita Tomeka is my new best friend."

"I do hope that you will get more than just information from her, Tíguere."

"Oh but of course. I have great plans for that filthy, unladylike mouth of hers," Zo smiled just as Meka returned to the table.

"Amorcita, what kept you so long?" Zo smiled at Meka.

"Oh nothing Papi, just some random ass bit–I mean, some girls in the restroom that have a problem with me," Meka huffed, switching her choice of words quickly to appease Zo's dislike of profanity. He'd told her numerous times that it was quite uncouth for her to curse so freely, and since she planned to sink her hooks deep into his pockets; she was determined to play the good girl role– whatever made him dish out the dick and cash.

"I hope that you did not stoop to their level…remember…always ladylike in the company of others," Zo playfully scolded her.

"I walked away Papi–proud of me?" Meka cooed as she planted her ample bottom in Zo's lap, leaning in to kiss his neck. Zo's hands immediately began their journey around her ass and up her hips. He shifted his posture to accommodate Meka's bodyweight on his lap; she continued to kiss her way up his neck, drawing his earlobe into her mouth with a playful nibble.

"Are you ladies enjoying yourselves?" Zo questioned Meka's two friends, who now sat on either side of his lieutenant.

"Yes!" they answered in unison. "Thank you for inviting us. No way we would have been able to get in without you hookin' us up," they smiled.

"It was my pleasure. And any friends of Señorita Tomeka's are friends of mine," Zo winked, taking a long drag from his Cuban before placing it in the ashtray. He then grabbed his glass and gulped down the last of his Remy XO. Meka continued to work her magic, giving Zo a subtle grind with just enough pressure to awaken his manhood. Eager to fuck the lining out of her pussy, Zo closed out his tab as the group gathered their things and headed for the front door. Meka made sure to walk on the far side of Zo, affording herself a perfect view of Chase and Kassidy while remaining hidden from their line of sight.

Chapter 18

After Kassidy's pep talk to Mia about Lando, Mia decided that Kassidy made a valid point, so she took her advice about taking things slow with Lando; she figured it couldn't hurt to see if she would get a different result–one other than her usual. Mia usually hooked up with ballers who were only attracted to her impressive body, and that were only interested in whisking her away to the nearest hotel to make her their smash of the night.

Mia and Lando got more acquainted after that night at his grand opening, and even though Lando had a wife at home, there was something about Mia that appealed to him–to both of his heads. Lando loved his wife like he'd never loved another, but Mia had a sassiness and quick wit about her that had him open–way more open than any married man should be with a chick other than his wife. His wife was the total opposite of Mia, and a welcomed break from the mini-storm that was brewing at his home now that the honeymoon period had worn off. Lando told Chase he was only interested in sleeping with Mia but after spending time with her, he found himself caught up in her web of sauciness.

"I'm glad you stopped by, L. I had a long day today, and you are just what I needed to unwind," Mia murmured, sliding next to Lando on her couch as she playfully slung her legs over into his lap.

"It's cool. I like kicking it with you too, ma. Why you makin' a nigga wait tho? Actin' like you don't wanna let me slide up in-between...I mean, you talk a good game and you say you like chilling, but every time we get something popping, you stop. What's up with that?"

"I don't know, L. See...I know you think you know me by all the shit you heard in them streets, but truth be told I'm kind of tired of the same ole shit. I need something a little more concrete. You know what I mean?"

"What you talking 'bout...relationship type shit?" Lando asked as he gave her a peculiar gaze. *Man, this ain't no love thing, shorty.*

"I don't know...maybe...yeah, kind of."

"Well, you know my situation ma. I'm not really in a position to give you that. I thought we would just kinda kick it, you know, have fun."

"Yeah I know, but I'm not talking about having a relationship with *you* specifically." Lando continued to give her a bizarre stare, not sure of exactly where the conversation was headed. "I'm just saying, that's what I want in general; you know, eventually one day," Mia continued.

"I feel you, baby girl. I'm sure every woman probably feels that way, right?"

"Not necessarily, it's just when you keep dating the same type of niggas, that shit gets old and played out. I'm looking for something different is all I'm sayin'."

"Is that right...well...I ain't sayin' I'm tryin' to be ya man or nothin, cuz like I already explained that's not somethin' I can't really give at this point, but I *can* show you something different, if you let me."

Mia smiled at Lando. *That's what the fuck I'm talking about, nigga. Show a bitch something different.* "You're are a total sweetheart you know that? Different from what I expected."

"I guess the streets got me wrong too then, huh?" Lando smirked.

"I guess so. They say you should never believe what you hear, and only half of what you see."

"Word."

Mia and Lando finished chatting it up while Mia's phone rang nonstop. When she saw that it was her ex DeMarco calling, she let his calls roll over to voicemail. Mia was more interested in what Lando had to offer, not listening to another one of DeMarco's lies he

was so comfortable with telling. Mia offered Lando something to drink, and he settled for an ice-cold Heineken.

Lando was right; Mia was definitely different from what he heard of her, but little did he know it was all an act. Mia had a plan to try to get him to fall head over heels for her, all so she could get in where she fit in with him and Chase's organization. Lando and Mia got lost in each other's company, and his phone rang right in the middle of them catching a laugh.

"Yo...what up?"

"Nigga why you sounding all jolly and shit? You must be deep off into some state-of-the-art pussy," Chase teased.

"Nah man, nothing like that, but definitely something I'm looking forward to."

"Sounds like a new bitch."

"Word."

Where you at bruh?" Chase chuckled, realizing Lando was with a new flame.

"On my way to meet up with you. I gotta run some shit down about some shit I found out about grand opening night."

"Aight...but why you just now speakin' on it nigga? I thought you was on top of shit."

"I am, but a nigga just got word of it myself."

"Aight nigga...I'll be leaving in about another hour or so; meet me at the spot."

"Word...I'll be there in a minute, I got a few stops to make first." While Lando and Chase ended their conversation, Mia took the opportunity to send DeMarco a quick text.

"Ay love...Imma go 'head and bounce. Make sure you tell that nigga you'll hit him back when I leave though. He interrupting my time right now."

Mia smiled at Lando recognizing she was texting another dude. She sat her phone down and leaned in, placing her lips on Lando's as they sucked each other faces.

"Damn, you sure you gotta leave already?" Mia whined, batting her thick lashes.

"Yeah man, I gotta go take care of something right quick."

"But I'm not ready for you to leave just yet," Mia said as she nibbled on his ear, placing small pecks on his neck.

"Give me a reason to come back then, because all you've been doing is teasing my dick and shit."

"I'll tell you this. When you do come back, if you decide to come back...I promise you not gonna wanna leave."

"Hmm…I like the way that sounds. I'll hit you when I'm on my way then."

"Okay daddi, you do that," Mia said as she kissed Lando one more time, making sure he left with her in his thoughts. As soon as Mia heard the sound of Lando's exhaust pipes leaving her apartment complex, she called DeMarco back.

"What's good?" DeMarco answered.

"I told you I was in the middle of something, why would you keep calling and shit?"

"I was tryna see what's up with what we talked about. Did you find anything out yet? You know a nigga's pockets hurtin' right now, and I can really use this come up to get back on my feet. The Feds took all my shit, you know that."

"Yeah I know, and that's what I was working on, but you blowing me up won't make shit go any faster. I told you Chase and his homies got a trip coming up soon. Calm down nigga and just wait for me to give you the when and where, damn."

"I am calm, but I need this shit to happen like ASAP, ya dig? Hit me up when everything's clutch."

"Will do DeMarco," Mia said as she tooted her lips and rolled her eyes to herself.

Chapter 19

While Lando was at Mia's getting ready to meet up with Chase, Chase was at home getting the silent treatment from Kassidy. Meka had been ringing Chase's phone all day, sending Kassidy back in her feelings about what happened with her at Lando's grand opening. She felt disrespected and made damn sure Chase was aware of her feelings. Kassidy thought Chase should have handled the situation with Meka differently. He promised her that he had cut all ties with the little sidepieces he had floating around Staten Island when the two of them became official. Kassidy felt that there must have been something still going on between the two of them for Meka to come for her the way that she did that night. Chase pleaded his case, but Kassidy wasn't buying it. She had already drawn her own conclusion.

"Listen, ma...I don't know what to tell you man. I didn't know that broad would even be there. That would be real stupid of me to invite some bitch I'm fucking with to the same place my woman would be, don't you think?"

Kassidy stood with her hands folded across her chest, mouth poked out as she stared at Chase. She was tired of talking about the incident, but wasn't fully convinced that Meka just so happened to show up at his homeboy's new spot just because she felt like it.

"Ma, don't just stand there, say something. I don't do silent treatments. Pressure bursts pipes, and if home ain't right, then what's the fucking point? Ma, I'm trying to rectify the situation, but it's like I'm talking to myself. I guess the apple don't fall to far from the tree based on what I seen with your daddy," Chase continued.

"Leave my daddy out of this, Chase. This is between you and me. I really don't have much to say. You said you didn't invite her, so you didn't invite her." Chase walked closer to Kassidy and placed his hand on the side of her face.

"You don't believe that yourself, because if you did then we wouldn't be still talking about this shit. I'm sorry, I shouldn't have brought your pops into this, but I need you to have a little more faith in *yo' man*. If I said I didn't invite that bitch there, I didn't invite her."

Kassidy inhaled deeply. She really wanted to believe Chase, but Meka's words hit her like a ton of bricks and got to her–whether she was willing to admit it or not. Kassidy wasn't the insecure type, but she knew Meka and other women were after what she had, and were willing to do anything to get it. It also didn't ease her mind knowing that Mia was there to remind her of just how much they wanted her man every chance she got.

"Did you love her, Chase? Is there any possibility that you may still be in love with that broad?" Chase lightly chuckled. "Oh you find my agony amusing?" Kassidy asked as she placed her hands on her hips, and her eyes narrowed.

"Nah ma, I don't find it amusing at all. I'm laughing because I can't believe you let that hoe get to you."

"Well you know what they say. When you lay with a hoe, you become her equal," Kassidy sassed.

"Awww, my baby is really mad with me. She taking jabs at her man and shit. Come here, ma," Chase said as he pulled Kassidy into his arms. "Listen baby...I'm not in love with that broad, and I've never been in love with her. She was just someone I fucked with– that's it. What her and I had is NOTHING compared to what we got. This the real deal right here.

"Promise?"

"Cross my heart and hope to die," Chase said as he did a kiddy expression of telling the truth by making a cross sign across his heart and kissing his finger. "I betcha she could never tell you or anyone else for that matter that she even knows what the inside of my crib looks like, and here you are posted up and shit."

Kassidy smiled. "Okayyyy...I believe you. I'm riding for you and only you; know that–and I shouldn't have to say that I expect the

same in return. If it's gonna be about us, then let it just be us. This ain't no community involvement type shit."

"I know that baby girl."

"I expect you to act like it then...now kiss me, silly."

"Are you sure, because you just called me a hoe on the sneak, and you know if you lay with me that makes you one too, right?" Chase joked.

"Only for you, my love. I'll be your hoe if that's what makes you happy."

"Only in the bedroom, baby girl. I leave them hoes on the corners, and I reign with Queens. You're my Queen, and don't you ever forget that ma," Chase affirmed as he leaned in and kissed Kassidy.

Chase lifted Kassidy up and placed her on the marble kitchen island. He raised her dress up and slid her thong to the side, and she became his meal of the day. Previous concerns about Meka melting away, Chase became the only thing that mattered to Kassidy. Make-up sex was Kassidy's reassurance that she had Chase's heart, and that everything he said about Meka was the absolute truth. They were over and there was no going back.

Chase's head resting comfortably in between Kassidy's thighs, Meka soon became an afterthought as Chase's kisses down low blew her mind. Kassidy pulled at his dreads as the force of his tongue sent her into an ecstatic heaven on earth. Her natural juices marinated his rugged beard as he plunged his tongue on her clit and rotated it up and down. Chase licked, pulled, and teased all around Kassidy's moist peach as she swirled her hips around in the figure eight motions.

"Ahhhh... mmmmm...baby yes...don't stop, please don't stop."

Chase continued to devour Kassidy creaminess as her body warned him she would soon explode. Her volcano was about ready to erupt, so he lifted his head and slid her rump to the edge of the countertop, pulled his manhood out, and slid deep into her

moistness. Chase held one of her legs up to his chest as the other rested on the Island. He placed his hand on the bottom of her back and dug deep as he could, stroking in and out, in and out of her. Kassidy's elbows rested on the counter for a minute, and then she lifted herself up and held Chase tightly around his neck. He continued to thrust inside of her, licking the side of her neck and placing wet kisses with his suckable lips.

"Fuck fuck fuckkkk! Ohhhhhhh shit! Harder baby harder, yes!" Kassidy screamed as her adrenaline pumped and her abdomen tightened.

Chase pumped faster and dug deeper into Kassidy's canal of love. He awakened her soul as he fiercely assaulted her walls. The intensity in her face told it all as her heart rate increased.

"Tell me this my dick daddi… tell me it's mine," Kassidy moaned.

"All yours baby. This dick is all yours," Chase growled his affirmation.

"Damn bae, shittttt…mmmm so good…I'm 'bout to cum baby."

"Let it go then ma… wet ya man up," Chase moaned as Kassidy's pussy tightened around his shaft. Her traction caused Chase's pipe to burst, sending a soaring flow deep inside of her. She embraced the thumping of his love muscle and tightened her kegels so they could thump together.

"Damn ma… fuckkkkkk! Mmmmm ahhhhh this some good fucking pussy," Chase uttered as he tried to hold steady and empty everything he worked up inside of her.

"Ohhhh Chaaaaase, yessss yesss," Kassidy moaned as she spasmed right along with Chase. Chase pulled her in close by the back of her head and passionately kissed her.

"I love you so much baby. You make me feel so damn good," Kassidy whispered. Chase smiled and kissed her one more time on her lips, and another on her forehead.

"Damn...I needed that quickie. I want some more of that good good when I get back. I gotta meet up with Lando in a minute." Kassidy slid her dress down and stepped down onto the floor as Chased reached out his hand to assist her.

"Hurry back babe. I wanna suck on my lollipop. You didn't even give me a chance," she teased.

"Don't worry, you can suck all night long when I get back. Damnnn, Lando's ass might have to wait because my dick just got hard again," Chase said as he stroked himself a few times.

"Go take care of your business bae, I'll be here when you get back."

"Fuck that! That nigga gon' have to wait. You should have never got me started," Chase said as he picked Kassidy up and escorted her into their shower. He ripped her dress off, and they stepped underneath the rainfall of water. Their passion for one another was undeniable. She gave Chase what the streets couldn't– real love, trust, and loyalty.

Kassidy took the sponge and quickly washed him off, then she got on her knees and slid his massive length into her mouth. Chase placed his hand to the back of her head as he moved it back and forth. The water drenched their bodies as their minds slipped into a mental oasis of their sexual bliss. Kassidy held his pipe in her mouth as she shook her head side to side at a steady pace. The edge of his dick grazed the root of her tongue as she continued to suck, jerking the base with her hand. Chase leaned his head back as the water hit his handsome face. *Damn baby, you suck me so fucking good.*

Kassidy maintained her lock on Chase's manhood with her soft lips as she placed her other hand in-between her legs. She caressed herself and started to moan as she held him inside her mouth. She bobbed her head back and forth as Chase continued to hold her at the back of her head. Her pace quickened until Chase unleashed his lava into her face. Kassidy licked the tip of his dick

until his seeds were all gone. She then got off her knees and embraced him.

"Damn ma, you da best," Chase uttered.

"I know," Kassidy winked as she reached for her sponge and body wash, and they showered together.

Damn I gotta make a move. I wonder what that nigga Lando was talking about when he said he had something to tell me about opening night. Fuck...nigga can stay in that pussy all day. Imma hit that shit again as soon as I get back.

Chapter 20

"Aight, run this shit down to me again," DeMarco prodded Mia, wanting to make sure he fully understood her offer.

"Damn nigga, you don't believe me or some shit? Look, one of my home girls is boo'd up with that nigga Chase now, and not on no random or side chick shit. That's wifey now, so she knows what moves he makes and when he makes 'em. So it's simple–we find out when and where their shipments come in, you get your team together and hit 'em, get the product and the cash, and there's your come up," Mia explained.

"So when you think you can get this info? Like how soon?"

"Shit, how soon you need it? Chase is havin' some kinda get together for his crew this weekend, so I can hit my girl up then," Mia assured DeMarco.

"See that's why I fucks with you ma, you stay lookin' out for a nigga and shit. Told you Imma give you the world baby girl; I'm 'bout to come up, real talk," DeMarco beamed, excited at what he was sure would be an easy payday. Little did Mia know, the only thing he planned on giving her was a good dickdown.

Having baited DeMarco sufficiently, Mia considered herself lucky to be able to make a quick exit without having to break him off with a mercy fuck. As Mia drove home from DeMarco's apartment, she couldn't contain the excitement at her new plan to claim her spot in Chase's inner circle. Deciding to try an alternate route from her usual thirst-trap ambitions, she figured she could more permanently solidify her spot in the circle by proving her loyalty, and who better to help her do that than DeMarco's snake ass? Setting him up to take the fall for trying to rob Chase was the perfect revenge for how he'd planned to let her rot in jail for catching a case meant for him. Now, all Mia had to do was find the perfect opportunity and delivery person to tip Chase off on DeMarco's plan; she figured if it came straight from her, then Chase would be suspicious right out the gate,

but coming from someone he trusted, he'd spring into action and rock DeMarco to sleep without a second thought.

***

More than ever, Chase had been having serious second thoughts about his newly acquired territory in St. Louis. It seemed like every time he turned around, there was another issue that pulled his and Lando's attention away from things on the Island. *Like a fuckin' toddler with ADHD or some shit,* Chase thought to himself as he mulled the situation. Based on the info Lando had just dropped on him, it looked like they'd be making yet another trip out that way, and he was less than enthused about having to break that news to Kassidy.

"So how the fuck that nigga Zo was able to slide up in yo' spot and ain't nobody know?" Chase quizzed Lando after learning that Zo had graced the grand opening with his presence.

"Fuck if I know, but I'm on it. Got some new niggas lined up to work the doors and shit. Can't stand a muthafucka that can't follow simple fuckin' instructions. If I say nobody gets in that ain't on the list, I mean no fuckin' body."

"And you say you positive that nigga ain't slide thru on some bogus name shit," Chase countered.

"My nigga I told you, everybody on the list, I knew 'em–not knew *of* them, but knew 'em. Damn right I'm positive."

"Aight, well we can tend to that shit when we get back. Let's make this run to the 'Lou and get the fuck back. Shit's ridiculous– you sure that nigga Cybo thorough like you say? Cuz right now that shit 'bout as rocky as a gravel pit and shit," Chase challenged Lando's suggestion to lead operations in St. Louis.

"Nigga, you know that cat Cybo is official. Ain't like he inherited no cake walk and shit either."

"Well he better figure some shit out quick, cuz a nigga feels like I got a long distance relationship with my girl's pussy and shit," Chase affirmed.

"You a fool wit it nigga, we out tho," Lando nodded as they pulled onto the tarmac and grabbed their duffels. They boarded the Gulfstream and settled in for the flight.

Hoping to avoid Kassidy's wrath since he wouldn't make it back to finish their session, Chase opted against a phone call and shot Kassidy a quick text to let her know about the impromptu trip. *She'll be calmed down by the time we touch down; I'll call her then,* he silently reasoned.

CHASE: *don't wait up ma. Issue out west, gotta head out & handle some shit. Hit u when we touch down.*

Not waiting for a response, Chase switched his phone to airplane mode, slid it back into his pocket, and sunk into the plush leather seat; within minutes of taking off, he'd drifted off to sleep.

*****

"Run that shit down again?" Chase prodded.

"I'm tellin' you, it was some synchronized shit, all the spots were hit at the same time. I'm tryin' to ring the soldiers and roll out Plan B, they ringin' my shit tellin' me they been hit. Crazy shit bruh," Cybo explained.

Before Chase had a chance to rip into Cybo and the others for, yet again, interrupting his evening plans to dick Kassidy down, he felt his phone buzzing an incoming message in his pocket. Muting Cybo with a raised index finger, Chase pulled the phone out, swiped to the message app, and opened the picture message. The sight staring back at him instantly had him on ten, his jaw clenched as his venomous anger boiled over.

***

Pissed about spending yet another night alone as Chase literally chased dollar signs out of state, Kassidy had drifted off into a restless sleep. Chase's last minute trip had her so thrown off that she neglected to make sure that the alarm was armed before she passed out for the night. Big mistake.

Parked in an empty driveway a few houses down, Zo smiled as he read the incoming text, confirming that the coast was clear.

"Move," Zo gave his driver the green light to ease up the street to Chase's house.

Exiting the vehicle quietly, Zo locked eyes with one of his men as he approached the front entry. With a slight head nod, the worker gave the go ahead for Zo to head inside.

"Yup," a second man whispered at Zo's visual cue, nodding his head toward the two duffels that rested to the side of the front door; he followed up with a second nod, indicating that Zo's target was upstairs. Returning the gesture, Zo made his way up the stairs, down the hallway, and toward the master suite, where yet another worker was posted up just outside the door.

Zo made entry, his footsteps muffled by the plush carpeting as he came face to face with a startled, yet sexy piece of temptation.

"Hola amorcita," Zo grinned, leaning down to lock eyes with the frightened doe sitting before him. Her curly mane sat wild atop her head, evidence of her sharply interrupted slumber. She struggled against her restraints, a scowl now settling on her face. After another few seconds of struggle, she abandoned her futile efforts, realizing her wrists and ankles were secured nice and tight. The cloth gag invading her mouth restricted her verbal options, so she redirected her attention to the unwelcomed intruder, never breaking their intense standoff gaze.

"King of Staten Island…untouchable they say," Zo prodded as he extended a hand to caress Ms. Temptation's cheek. "Feel safe?" he continued, receiving no reaction from his hostage.

"Tell you what…I'm not a total brute…and that lovely face is much too beautiful to bring harm to…so how about we just play a little game of messenger," Zo leaned closer into her face as he filled his lungs to capacity with an inhalation of the light fragrance that graced her neck. Brushing his cheek against hers, he brought his left hand up at the same moment that he planted his lips into the softness of her cheek. Snapping a quick selfie with Ms. Temptation, he slipped the phone into his pocket before he continued.

"Messenger…are you willing to make a special delivery?" Zo hissed as his worker's weapon remained trained on Ms. Temptation's head. "Untouchable is usually just a state of mind, an illusion of security for the weak, and the weak will crumble with ease. Let the Staten Island's Finest know that I can touch him anywhere…and everywhere at the same time…including…here…" Zo smirked as he dipped his hand between Kassidy's legs. His palm slid further up her thigh, pausing as his fingertips reached her moist center. This brought a falter to Kassidy's previously stoic scowl as her eyes grew wider with fear.

"No worries…I'm not a man that has to *take*…especially since you'll give it willingly sooner than you realize," Zo continued to taunt. "Let the *King of Staten* Island know that it would be in his best interest to stick to just that–Staten Island. If not, I'm fairly certain that my next visit will leave him less enthused…although it will bring you a great deal of pleasurable pain, *Amorcita*."

Throwing a wink in Kassidy's direction as he retreated from the room, Zo nodded to each of his workers as he descended the stairs and headed out the front entry, returning to his waiting vehicle.

Following previous orders, Zo's workers loosened Kassidy's restraints and made their own retreat, having given her strict orders not to move until the landline phone on the nightstand rung.

Exiting the residential neighborhood and heading toward the highway, Zo read the "all clear" text from his men, indicating that they'd successfully departed Chase's home, duffel bags in tow. Zo's lips curled into a sinister smirk as he scrolled to the pictures of Kassidy, including their impromptu selfie, he selected the group of photos, attached them to a message, and hit send. Screen displaying a confirmation of successful transmission, Zo removed the SIM card and tucked it into his breast pocket, lowered the window, and tossed the burner phone out the window. A steady flow of traffic crushed the phone under a flurry of Firestones.

Chapter 21

"Calm down, calm down ma...no...okay ma...right...no–stay right where you are, Rick's on the way over now...no, he won't need you to–look, I'm leaving now, I'm on my way back bae...I love you, ma," Chase struggled to keep his tone mellow while easing Kassidy's nerves. Truthfully, he was on ten and ready to body everything moving on the Island once he touched down. *Knew some shit ain't feel right*, he huffed to himself.

After getting the rundown from Kassidy on how Zo had the balls to set foot in his home, Chase left Lando to handle things in St. Louis and hopped the jet back to NY. He felt like shit for her being dragged into the situation with Zo, and he just hoped he could put an end to it all and get to Zo before he could try some more slick shit. Chase trusted Lando with his life, but he was a little too laid back for him in some situations, like the mishaps that kept popping up in St. Louis. Luckily for everyone, Kassidy's call had interrupted his tirade, because he was literally two seconds from bodying the entire crew out there, including Cybo.

Hoping Lando handled shit the boss way, Chase shifted his thoughts back to Kassidy. Aside from his money, she'd been his main priority, and he couldn't help feeling he'd failed her. Clenching his jaw as he popped his knuckles, he committed that the money would have to come in second as he turned his full focus to Kassidy and making sure she felt safe. He made a mental note to hit his realtor up and start house hunting.

No doubt about it, Zo was sending a clear message to Chase, letting him know that nothing was off limits, and that he could touch him anywhere, and especially where he was most vulnerable–his woman. He still drew a blank mentally as he tried to figure out how he didn't see the shit with Zo coming. True enough, he agreed to the deal with Mark largely off the premise that they went way back, but

he knew better than to take any nigga at his word, a grave mistake he was now paying the price for.

Chase thought about just saying fuck it and walking away from St. Louis, but resigned he couldn't do it for two reasons–one, he was nobody's bitch and refused to let a nigga send him running; and two, he couldn't turn his back on all that money. Life in the Midwest must have been either really boring or really slow, because he had a hard time keeping his spots stocked with product; they were always down to their last bricks when the shipments came in.

When the jet landed, Chase jumped into his truck and did a hundred on the freeway to try to get to Kassidy. He phoned her to make sure she was all right, but he could barely understand her because she was distraught. He pulled into his neighborhood and sped down the road that led to his house. Reaching the driveway, he jumped out of his vehicle and ran inside.

"Kass! Kass! Where you at!" Chase yelled as he walked through the house looking for Kassidy. She never answered him, so he ran up to the bedroom. He glanced around the room when he walked in, realizing Kassidy was packing a tote bag.

"Babe...what are you doing? Are you okay?" he asked as he pulled her away from the dresser and pulled her into his arms. Kassidy laid into his chest as a few tears fell from her eyes.

"Kass, you okay? Did that nigga hurt you?" Chase asked as he examined her from head to toe, and then back up to her face. He wiped her flood of tears.

"Yeah bae...I'm fine. It's just...I can't believe this happened. I mean, who are they, Chase? What do they want?" Chase took Kassidy by her hand and led her over to their bed.

"Sit down ma, everything is gon' be alright, okay? I'm just glad you're okay baby. I came as soon as I got the message.

"Chase...how do you know that? You don't know that for sure–you can't possible know if everything is gonna be okay. I mean...they came in our fuckin' house! I'm supposed to be able to feel safe at home. That shit scared the fuck out of me. Can you

imagine how I felt? I mean, do you have any idea how it feels to have a gun pointed at you in your home?"

"I'm sorry Kass, I really am. It won't happen again, I promise."

"I don't know babe...I mean...maybe I should just go back to my house for a while. Like, just until this gets under control."

"No, you ain't going nowhere! I'm not about to have you out there like that–besides, I can't protect you if you there and I'm here. Ain't happenin'."

"But you weren't even here and it DID happen, Chase!"

Chase stared at Kassidy. It killed him to see her shaken up by something that could have been prevented–so he thought so anyway. He felt disrespected, violated, and had it in for Zo big time. Never in a million years did Chase think anybody would have been bold enough to cross him in that way. Chase wasn't the one to fuck with, and everyone knew that but Zo. Zo was in a league of his own, and he wasn't afraid to test Chase's street cred. Zo was all for pushing boundaries and testing waters that he eventually and always ended up treading. Lorenzo Valentino was a name that rang in the streets of the Dominican Republic, and with a reach that extended into the States, he was definitely a force to be reckoned with–something Chase was going to learn one way or another.

"Listen ma, I know this really freaked you out, but know that nothing like this will ever happen again. That nigga caught me slipping cuz I had to ride out at the last minute. I know for sure I won't give him that opportunity again. You stayin' right here so I can make sure that shit don't happen again. I know that nigga hit my stash for some stacks, but I ain't trippin' off that–that shit don't matter at the end of the day. It can be replaced, but you can't."

"But what if he comes back, Chase?"

"He won't."

"That's not what he said."

Chase raised his eyebrows and looked at Kassidy oddly. "What you mean?"

"He told me to give you a message."

Chase abruptly stood to his feet. He paced the floor for a second and then he stood still in front of Kassidy. "You mean to tell me, that bitch ass nigga actually told you to relay something to me." *This motherfucker's dick must be bigger than his brains. I gotta lullaby his ass.*

"Yeah he did. He said something like, 'let the king of Staten Island know he should just stick to Staten Island.'"

In that moment, Chase realized he shouldn't take Zo's threat lightly, and he shouldn't put anything past him. Breaking into his crib and stealing money was one thing, but taunting his woman was another. The writing was on the wall, and Chase knew Zo wasn't bluffing.

"He say anything else?"

"Not really...oh um...something 'bout you'll be less enthused about his next visit."

"Oh that nigga think he gon' run up in my shit again!" Chased boomed. He was pressing Kassidy for more details, not because he was worried about Zo returning, but because he had every intention in making Zo regret that he ever came for him.

"Yeah pretty much, that's what he said. You never answered me–who is he? And what does he want?"

"Nothing for you to worry about, ma. I told you I'll take care of it and I will."

Kassidy stood to her feet, and her eyes met Chase's. "Don't do that. Tell me who he is. I have a right to know, don't you think? I mean even if I stay–"

"Which you WILL stay. I mean what I say, Kass," Chase interrupted.

"Okay...I'll stay, but as I was saying...I should know who he is at least. I can't just stay locked away, I do work. What if I run into him on the street or something?"

"You won't. He ain't even the type you just run into on the street. His name is Lorenzo. He goes by Zo or some shit. Like I said,

it's really not nothing you should concern yourself with, ma. This shit was about turf. Don't think I'm just brushin' it off though. Ain't no nigga 'bout to get away with running in my shit and live to talk about it."

"Okay, now you're telling too much," Kassidy weakly smiled.

"Well I tried to keep it to myself, but you wouldn't let it go. Did the alarm go off?"

"Well umm...I kinda forgot to arm it. After I got out of the shower, I watched a little television. After I got your text about leaving, I guess I got in my feelings and forgot about it all together."

"Kass, baby...you can't let that happen again. You gotta remember to arm the system. I mean, that's what I got it for–to help keep shit secured, especially when I'm away."

"I'm sorry babe, it won't happen again," Kassidy said as she started to feel a bit guilty, and put her head down. Kassidy realized that if she would have set the alarm, maybe the incident may not have even happened. Chase noticed the change in her face.

"Come here, ma," Chase said as he pulled Kassidy into his chest. "None of this is your fault. We just have to be a lil more careful and be on top of shit so something like this don't happen again. Don't worry, I'm not gon' let anything happen to you, I gotchu. The nigga wanted my attention and now he got it. I gotchu, okay love?"

Chase consoled Kassidy as he plotted his next move. He got Zo's message loud and clear, and he planned to clap back with an even louder message in return. Since that nigga supposedly had shit on lock in the DR and decided to so disrespectfully run up in his shit, Chase pondered the possibility of going at Zo in the same way–hitting close to home, on his own turf.

Thinking back over everything he'd handled in the past few months, Chase felt like his plate had runneth over. It seemed like he had niggas coming at him from every direction, trying to test him and steal what he'd worked so hard for. He needed to kick some shit

to Lando and see how they could switch some things up and add some more men to their team. Chase had every intention of keeping his promise to Kassidy, and keeping her out of harm's way. His eyes were wide open now, and Kassidy was now his main focus.

Chase was far from scared after Zo's little stunt, but he definitely intended to address it. Ain't no way in hell he was going to let Zo and his clique run him out of business. Chase wasn't known for being a hothead for no reason; the spitting image of his Haitian father, his blood ran deep through his veins, and there wasn't a bitch or nigga alive who could put fear in his heart. He was really going to need Lando to step up and help him juggle shit, so he hoped Lando was up for the challenge.

Lando, nigga, you BETTER be on top of shit like you keep saying you are because from the looks of it, you slipping big time homie. I need a gorilla, not a motherfucking finger monkey who keeps holding them niggas hands and shit. Either you made for this shit or you not.

Chapter 22

Meka gave herself one last spot-check in the mirror, pressing her lips together to ensure even distribution of her Brave Red Guo Pei by MAC. As much as her lips longed for a taste of Zo, Chase was a flavor she'd forever crave. Meka had worked her brain overtime for the past few months, with much prodding from Zo, to figure out a way to lure Chase back between her thighs. True enough, they were never exclusive, but Meka never really expected Chase to diss her for a permanent replacement. Chase Baptiste didn't do commitment–everyone knew that–so the fact that Ms. Kassidy was able to snag something no other chick on the Island had succeeded at had Meka even more determined to break up their happy little home.

Being a rising player in Staten Island's real estate game afforded Meka an opportunity to see how the other half lived. Every open house left her even thirstier for her slice of the pie of success– not to mention, she got to rub elbows with all sorts of masculine deliciousness, especially considering the clients of her firm's commercial division. Meka knew that Chase had dealings with a senior realtor at the firm, and after a bit of covert snooping, she'd found the perfect ploy to pull Chase back into her web–and complete what Zo asked of her.

Confident that her looks were up to par, Meka grabbed her keys, purse, and phone before heading out the door. Sliding her Ray Bans into place, she winked at her reflection in the visor mirror before exiting the parking lot of her complex, speeding off toward her meeting in the Crookes Point area.

Pulling into the makeshift parking area before her client arrived, Meka parked, pressed the ARM button on her key fob, and stepped up the graveled path toward the building's entry. Meka usually handled residential showings, so she felt a bit out of her element in the abandoned industrial park–but the small measure of

discomfort was worth it when the caveat was a snippet of one-on-one time with Staten Island's finest.

Just as she had completed a cursory walkthrough of the open space, Meka's attention was pulled to the sound of gravel crunching underneath a set of tires. Click-clacking her heels across the cement slab floor, Meka paused just beyond the entry as her client stepped inside.

"Fuck is goin' on–look, a nigga ain't got time for your bullshit, Meka."

"Well hello to you too Chase–and relax, this is all business. Scott asked me to fill in for one of his agents," Meka explained with a sly smile.

"I bet. Ay, have him hit me up when his regular gets back," Chase quipped as he turned to leave.

"Wait! Look, you drove all the way out here to see the place, right? So then see it–all bullshit aside, strictly business," Meka rebutted as she slipped into full business mode, catching Chase off guard.

Bitch really is about her business...okay, let's see how this plays out, Chase reasoned after briefly weighing whether he should be alone with Meka after Kassidy's previous rant. *It's just business,* he told himself before following Meka for a quick tour of the spot he was considering for purchase.

Fifteen minutes later, Chase found himself thoroughly impressed with Meka's skills. She was legit a shark in the real estate game, putting any concern that he shot her way about the property to rest. Add the fact that her pencil skirt seemed to be caught in a tug of war with her bountiful ass that threatened to betray every stitch in the seam, and Chase couldn't keep his eyes off Meka. Sure, Kassidy made it known where his interest should be, but there was nothing wrong with looking, right?

"So the asking price is 1.3 mil. I'm not sure who you've secured for financing, but I'd recommend coming in slightly under asking with your initial bid. This property has been on the market for

some time, and though 1.3 mil is a steal, the owner is ready to move quickly," Meka continued her professional facade, thumbing through the papers in her folder as she caught Chase checking her out in her peripheral.

"Slightly under huh…so how much should I make the check out for?" Not surprised that he'd be paying in cash, Meka maintained her composure.

"You give me a number, I'll get it back to the owner, and if all goes well, you'll have keys in hand within the next 48 hours."

"Word. Hook it up," Chase instructed, still a bit shocked that Meka hadn't tried to throw herself at him yet.

"I'll get right on it. And is this still a good number to reach you at?" Meka questioned, extending the showing request form for Chase's review; Chase nodded his confirmation.

"Perfect…umm before you go…" Meka began as she stuffed the folder into her Burberry attaché. "About that thing at Premier…look, my fault…you know I don't even usually get down like that. I was just a little lifted, in full turn-up mode and…yeah, I just got a little carried away. You know I've held you down for a minute, and I got nothing but respect for you…and I'm not gonna lie, it felt foul as fuck seeing you all boo'd up with 'ol girl…but I still respect you…which means I gotta respect her…so again, I apologize. Friends?" Meka extended her hand with a sad pout resting on her face.

Fuck kinda game this bitch tryin' to play, Chase mused as he pondered the ulterior motive behind Meka's newfound remorse. "You know I'ont really do friends, ma," Chase spoke.

"Come on Chase…nooooo I'm not tryin' to fuck you…noooo I'm not tryin' to sneak diss your girl… real talk, I just wanna put it in the past and keep it movin'…no reason we can't squash everything like adults, right?"

"Aight, accepted, that's what's up. I gotta dip though," Chase retrieved his keys and activated his remote start.

"Wait! How about a quick drink… you know, to celebrate all this," Meka extended her arms and gave the surrounding space an all-encompassing glance.

Chase hesitated for a moment at her invitation. *We could stick to a spot out the way…it's public…and it's just a drink…and she did pull some strings to get me a showing on short notice…fuck it.*

"One drink girl…no slick shit either…I swear Meka, I ain't with the dumb shit," Chase called over his shoulder as he exited the building. A sneaky smile spread across Meka's face as she jumped for joy inside. *Easier than I thought it'd be.*

***

True to his word, Chase followed Meka to Miller's Ale House and joined her for a drink. Fortunately, his phone provided just the right amount of distraction to keep things from getting too deep or going too far left with Meka. She was slick as fuck, and Chase knew all too well how they could be kicking it one minute, with the tip of his dick tickling her tonsils the next.

Lando had been texting some numbers for Premier's first celebrity VIP event, so Chase had been preoccupied for much of his time there with Meka.

"So what are your plans for the space? Kinda dead and out in the middle of nowhere, don't you think?" Meka quizzed but before he could respond, Chase's phone jingled an interruption via an incoming call.

"Ay ma, I gotta take this real quick, hold tight," Chase broke in before stepping off toward the rear of the bar, where there was a bit less noise. Seizing her opportunity, Meka quickly retrieved a vial from the inner pocket of her Burberry clutch. Drawing the liquid into the medicine dropper, she quickly released the fluid into Chase's Red Stripe beer. Returning the vial to her clutch, she swirled his beer around for a few seconds, placing the beer back into its resting spot just as Chase rounded the corner to return to his seat.

"Everything okay?" Meka feigned interest.

"Yeah I'm straight, just business," Chase replied before turning the bottle up and draining the remainder of its contents to quench his thirst.

Feeling more relaxed as the minutes ticked by, Chase and Meka fell into a more flirtatious conversation. Half an hour later, Chase was loose and limber, just as Meka intended. Convincing him that he was too inebriated to drive, she offered him her couch for the evening to sleep off his intoxication. Unable to put up much of a protest, Chase conceded, passing Meka his keys for the short drive to her condo down the street. Glancing at Chase from the driver seat, Meka's devilish smirk grew as she thought about what she had in store for him. *Yeah, we gon' see if you be callin' wifey's name tonight,* she laughed inwardly.

Chapter 23

"Cybo, you know you my man a hundred grand, but this shit foul as fuck. If you can't handle it and shit, then speak up my nigga. Ain't gon' be too much more of me keepin' that nigga Chase off y'all asses," Lando emphasized.

"I got this shit nigga, this is just residuals from that fraud ass nigga Mark and the shit he got boppin' in the streets," Cybo reasoned.

"I ain't hearin' shit but excuses bruh. Shit, you already a pass in the red with that nigga Chase. Now I gotta try to smooth this shit ova when I touch down so he don't come back out here and clean house, lay all y'all niggas down."

"I hear you L… good lookin' out tho," Cybo conceded.

"Real talk, you betta hope them niggas in yo' crew official…only as strong as ya weakest link, bruh, remember that. Aight tho, I'm out," Lando gave Cybo a head nod as he left the warehouse, climbed in his rental, and sped off toward the Hilton.

Pulling into the hotel's parking lot about 45 minutes later, Lando snatched up his phone on his way inside. It buzzed yet again as he stepped onto the elevator with another message from Mia. Shorty was cool and all, but she was in full bugaboo mode as she blew his phone up.

Sliding his room key into the reader, he slipped his Timbs off and pulled his hoodie over his head, tossing it onto the chaise. *Lemme get this chick out the way for the night*, he sighed as he shot Mia a text.

LANDO: *You up*
MIA: *You know it, call me hun*
LANDO: *Dressed?*
MIA: *Y? U tryin' 2 phone bone?*

Fuckin' tease, Lando chuckled as he rubbed his groin, feeling it grow at just the thought of digging Mia's pussy out.

LANDO: *Ma u wildin', get on FaceTime.*

Just as Lando settled into the king-sized bed and posted up against the headboard, his phone flashed an incoming FaceTime call.

"What's good ma?"

"Hey boo, what you been up to? I tried to hit you earlier," Mia beamed.

"Ain't shit ma, makin' moves, handlin' business, you know how we do. What's good tho?"

"Umm, when you comin' back? I need to kick it to you about something important," Mia pouted.

"Tell me now ma, what's up?"

"Umm...I kinda need to tell you face to f–"

"I don't do surprises ma, so you gon' need to go 'head and lemme know what's up," Lando pressed; Mia exhaled a sharp sigh before continuing.

"Umm...I'm not tryin' to have Chase after me...but I heard something about his business...and I kinda think he would want to know. I know he don't exactly think I'm–"

"You talkin in circles ma, just run it to me. What's the deal?"

"Well...I know this guy from around the way...DeMarco...and I kinda overheard him talking about some stuff he has planned. I heard something about Chase, a drop, a shipment, and some other stuff. I don't know if he was just talkin' shit or if it's legit, but I thought I should let you know," Mia began. Lando crossed his arms across his chest and put his poker face on display, determined to shield his feelings as Mia continued.

"How you say you know this cat again?"

"Oh, he's just this dude from around the way. I don't really *know him* know him, I just kinda know of him," Mia stammered, trying to hide the nervousness of her lie. Lando sat quiet for a

minute, letting Mia's words swim through his head as he decided what to do with the info.

"Aight ma...that it?"

"Yeah, pretty much. But you know I'll let you know if I hear anything else around the way," she smiled, still unsure of how to read Lando's stoic facial expression.

"Word. Ay, I gotta handle somethin' right quick. Imma get at you in a lil bit ma."

"Okay, so you gonna—" but Lando disconnected the FaceTime session before Mia could finish.

Dropping his phone to the bed, Lando swiped his hand down from forehead to chin, then reached up to rub his waves as he thought about the details that Mia had just dropped on him. He'd heard DeMarco's name before, but as far as he knew, the dude was just a small-time wannabe that ran his mouth too much to be taken seriously by even the most amateur corner boys.

Beyond exhausted from all the recent trips between the Island and St. Louis, Lando stripped down and climbed into the shower. The temperature was scalding, just how he liked it, and soothed his achy muscles to set him up for what he hoped would be a restful night of sleep. Lando fell into deep thought, thinking about how he had been making most of the St. Louis trips alone; Chase wanted to stick close to home in light of Zo's recent stunt. Nothing messed with a man's head more than feeling like he couldn't hold things down at home, which included protecting his family from outside threats.

Shower complete, he dried off and slipped on a pair of boxers, basketball shorts, and a wife beater before shooting Chase a quick text to check in. Next, he texted his wife that he'd call her the next day before he crawled under the covers and knocked out for the night.

***

While Chase was having drinks and talking real estate with Meka, Kassidy and Mia were talking lingerie on Facetime as Mia got ready for her date with Lando. Mia was satisfied that she'd held out long enough and planned to serve up some toe-curling pussy the next time Lando stopped through later. She wanted her outfit to walk the fine line between freak and thot, so she asked Kassidy for her input.

"Girl uh, that shit says turnt up THOT–no, try again," Kassidy frowned at Mia in her iPad screen.

"Damn K, what the fuck? I ain't tryin' to be Mother Theresa and shit! You don't like nothin'!"

"Mia, I'm just tryin' to school your thot ass a lil bit, but you can be one of the ratcheteers if that's the look you goin' for. You gotta stop thinking like you messing with one of these broke ass bums. A real man likes to unwrap his gift…that's part of the allure of it all. Just try it, you'll have Lando lookin' for your ass in the daytime with a flashlight," Kassidy winked, slurping up the last of her green smoothie.

"Ewe, I don't see how you drink that seaweed soup shit!" Mia grimaced.

"Shut up heifer, it ain't soup and it's good for you. You always talking 'bout your abs are hidden under your gut, you need to get your ass on this green life and skip that drive thru once in a while."

"I know right? But it works wonders for all this ass," Mia joked as she turned her back to the camera and twerked a few times in Kassidy's face.

"Ugh, get yo' life! I gotta go anyway–bye tramp!"

"Wait Kass before you go. Are you really okay? Man, I can't believe some niggas ran up in Chase's shit like that and you were there. I know I would have been scared as fuck if it were me."

"Yeah girl, I'm good. After that happened, you know he got all kind of security and shit running all up and around here. I don't think them fools that stupid to come back here."

"Yeah, you probably right. If they know like I know, they fucking with the right one fucking with Chase Baptiste. Mister Trigger Finger himself.

"I know right," Kassidy said as her mind briefly drifted back to that night, causing her to cringe.

"Well I'm glad you're okay mami and nothing crazy happened. So now back to Lando's fine ass. He definitely better know how to make a bitch bend over and touch her toes, because if he ain't working with nothing, Imma be like…I'll holla."

"Bye Mia," Kassidy laughed and shook her head as she ended the chat session and shifted her attention to her phone, which had just buzzed with an incoming message from a number she didn't recognize.

Raising her body in her seated position on the bed, Kassidy opened the message and waited for the video to buffer. A few seconds later, she felt a wave of sickness and anger simultaneously wash over her body as she gawked at the contents of the video.

"Fuuuuuuck Chase shiiiiiit, I luv dis dick! I luv dis dick! This my shit! Tell me this my shit!"

"All you, ma…this all you, ma…fuck…spread that shit ma…spread that fuckin' pussy open girl…" Chase groaned his pleasure as he gripped the chick's hips and took control of her wild attempt to ride him. As she locked her ankles around his thighs, Chase commenced to a merciless pounding of her pussy. The chick's ass pounded out an up-tempo rhythm as it smacked against Chase's thighs. Kassidy's eyes remained fixed on her phone, which shook in the trembling grip of her left hand. Just when she thought she'd seen enough, Chase and his co-actress decided to bless her with a grand finale.

"Chaaaaase…shit…Chaaaase…I'm bout to cum bae……ahhhhhh."

"Shit, let it go ma…let that shit go…ahhhhhhh," Chase groaned, tightening his grip on the chick's voluminous hips as his own orgasm began to wash over his body.

Kassidy's eyes locked on Chase's next two abbreviated thrusts, which were followed by one long, sustained pump as he no doubt emptied his semen deep into the girl's pussy. Having seen enough, Kassidy threw her phone against the headboard. She stood frozen in place for a moment, a mix of shock, disgust, and rage taking up residence next to her rapid heartbeat.

Snapping out of her trance, Kassidy swiftly crossed the bedroom floor, snatching the door open and stepping into their shared walk-in closet. She grabbed her PINK gym bag and stuffed a few outfits inside. Snatching their center closet island open, she grabbed a few undergarments and stuffed them in the bag as well.

Next, she exited the closet, stuffed her phone and charger into her Chanel Trolley bag, and raced down the stairs, eager to get the fuck up out of Chase's crib.

"Dog ass nigga, uuuuuugggggghhh!" she screamed as she dragged her bags down the stairs, struggling not to trip.

"Ms. Kassidy, you know we can't let you leave," one of the bodyguards Chase had watching her cut her off at the foot of the stairs.

"Rick, get the fuck outta my way, I'm not trying to hear that shit!" she snapped.

"All due respect baby girl, but since I know you can't kick my ass, yo' tantrum ain't fazing me. I'm much more worried about NOT catchin' a bullet from Chase," Rick asserted.

"Rick…get…the…fuck…out…of…my…FUCKIN…WAY, " Kassidy countered, pulling the Beretta Pico that Chase made her keep within arm's reach since Zo's surprise visit a few weeks earlier.

"Oh you serious ma…aight…can you just call Chase before you go so he won't—"

"Get the fuck on Rick!" Kassidy shrieked as she blazed past him, out the door and to her car. Throwing her bags in the back seat, she shifted into drive and spun up a cloud of dust and loose gravel as she burned rubber out of Chase's driveway.

Making a right turn off Chase's road, she pulled over to the side of the road to dig her phone out of her Chanel bag. Just as she brought it out to sync it with her in-dash Bluetooth....

BAM!

"What the fuck!" she screeched, throwing her car into park as she threw the door open. She stomped toward her rear bumper just as an all-black, tinted out Suburban charged toward her, coming to a screeching halt right alongside her car. Before she could react or reach for her Beretta, she felt a bag coming down over her head as she was snatched up and thrown into the back of the SUV, her phone slipping from her hand and crashing to the pavement in the process.

Chapter 24

Waking up the next morning, Chase shot up from his supine position on Meka's couch, unable to remember much of anything. *The fuck I end up here?* He glanced down and found himself clothed in nothing but his Ralph Lauren boxers, a black wife beater, and some socks. *Please tell me I ain't fuck this bitch.* He noticed his clothes neatly folded on the arm of the couch and frowned in confusion, really puzzled as to how he ended up in the one place Kassidy would likely kick his ass for being at.

"Fuck, Kassidy," Chase panicked, reaching for his jeans and hoping Meka hadn't done anything foul with his phone. Surprised to find the phone neatly tucked in his pocket, Chase pressed the home button to find that he had nine missed calls and 14 missed texts. "Shit," he hissed as his mind shifted into high gear, already working to spin an excuse for not going home the night before. Just as he reached the last unread text, Meka appeared in the living room.

"I thought I heard you stirring in here," Meka smiled as she pulled her Victoria's Secret robe tight around her wide hips and tied the belt to ensure its closure.

"Uhh hey...umm, how did I–"

"Calm down. You were a little too gone last night, and I couldn't just sit by and let you wrap your truck around a pole. Here," Meka swiped his keys from one of the side tables and dangled them from her finger.

"Good lookin' out ma," Chase breathed a sigh of relief. Meka was always extra touchy feely the morning after a dick down, so Chase took comfort in the fact that she seemed to be too calm to be fresh off his dick. He didn't think his balls felt extra light either. "Ay, I gotta rip though," Chase huffed as he hurriedly dressed and slid his feet into his Timbs.

"Sure. Umm, I'll give you a call when I hear back from the owner?"

"Fa sho. Aight ma, be easy," Chase called over his shoulder as he pulled Meka's door closed behind him. Meka skipped back to her bedroom and grabbed her phone up off the nightstand. Opening the line to #4 in her speed dial entries, she waited for the call to connect; she piped up when the call was answered on the third ring.

"It's done," Meka smiled before disconnecting the call. Falling back onto her bed, she folded her arms and locked her fingers behind her head, feet dangling a few inches above the floor. *Like I said nigga, you know where home is*, Meka smiled.

***

Having temporarily smoothed things out in St Louis, Lando hopped an early flight back to Staten Island, but instead of returning to his not so happy home with his wife, he headed over to Mia's place. He knew she was looking forward to seeing him, and he could only imagine just how she intended to show how much she missed him. Lando hadn't heard from Chase as of yet, so neither he nor Mia had any idea that Kassidy was missing.

Lando got some shuteye after his conversation on Facetime with Mia, but he couldn't help but think about the bomb she dropped on him about that nigga DeMarco and his plans to try to come up at their expense. Lando couldn't wait to kick what he heard to Chase, but first he had to get a taste of Mia's sweetness before he did anything.

Finally back in NY, Lando grabbed a cab and left the airport, heading to pick up his car so he could make moves. He eased his cell from his pocket and immediately dialed Mia.

"Yeah," Mia answered in a low croaky tone as she was just turning over in her king-sized bed.

"Get up, sleepy head. I just touched down and I'm headed your way."

"Hey boo...ohhh okay, I'm getting up now," Mia whispered as she glanced at the time on her cell phone. "Damn...it's only 5:30. I

don't have to be to work 'til nine," Mia yawned as she thought about whether she'd go in early that day or not.

"I hear you, but work is the last thing I got on my mind. What you got on, sexy?"

Mia lightly snickered. "Mmm, something I'm sure you'll like," she said as she slid her hand slowly across her chest, rubbing her breasts and resting her hand on her neck.

"I hope so, ma. See you in a few."

Once their call ended, Mia got up and went into the bathroom. She brushed her teeth and washed her face. She was already showered and primed from last night. She took her scarf off her head and ran her fingers through her hair so that her curls wouldn't appear flat. She reached into the drawer of her vanity mirror and fetched her powder puff, and then swiped it across her face. She made sure it didn't appear as though she had any makeup on. Mia also saturated her lips with lip balm so they would feel soft and smooth when Lando kissed her. She thought it was too early to beat her face in full make-up, so she settled for a natural look instead. Mia wanted Lando to think she really woke up like that. She placed her hands inside of her chest, fixing her breasts and making sure her girls fit securely in the cups of the black lacy chemise that showed everything.

Of course, Mia ignored Kassidy's advice and left nothing to the imagination; her chemise showed nipples and all. She lifted her breasts up one by one, damn near making them spill over the top; she then pinched her own nipples to make them erect. Mia's girls were sitting pretty. Satisfied that she was serving up maximum fuckability, she headed back to her bedroom where she slipped into her Boudoir furry slippers by Frederick's of Hollywood. *You have no idea how bad I want to fuck you, and I hope me listening to Kass has changed your perception of me. It's showtime; I've waited long enough*, Mia thought to herself. As Mia took one last glance in the mirror, her doorbell rang. She strutted to the door and peeked out of

her peephole. She noticed it was Lando, and a big Kool-Aid smile stole across her face.

"Damn ma, mmm..." Lando said, pure lust invading his wide eyes as he bit his bottom lip. Mia just stood in the door with her hand on her hip and smiled. Lando's facial expression told her that he was just as happy to see her assets as she was to see him.

"Good morning," Mia said as she grabbed Lando by the hand and escorted him into her bedroom.

"Oh yeah, it's def a good morning," Lando happily responded as he let Mia lead him into her bedroom.

Lando didn't waste any time and quickly stripped out of his clothing, laying Mia onto her bed. He and Mia finally got the chance to explore each other, something both of them had been looking forward to. Mia made sure she put it on Lando too, just to make sure he would come back for more. Lando's mind was blown and he enjoyed every bit of Mia's yoga and twerking moves. She was very flexible–so much so that she could have been a gymnast.

After two hours of huffing, puffing, licking, and sucking, Mia had sweated her curls out, and her and Lando were both exhausted––a good kind of tired though. Mia laid across his chest with the biggest smile on her face.

"I gotta get up and make some moves ma. I wish I could stay a lil bit longer with you, but you know how it is. Nah mean?"

"Yeah, I know. I got shit to do too–one of them being getting ready for work."

"I feel ya but before I go...run that down to me again what you was telling me about ol' boy."

"Oh yeah...about that," Mia said as she sat up to make sure Lando heard every word she said about DeMarco's plan to rob them.

Mia ran it down verbatim, and Lando couldn't wait to inform Chase of DeMarco's idea to hit a lick, courtesy of them. Lando paid close attention to every word Mia said and thanked her for telling him. He then jumped in her shower and returned to the room with Mia still laying in her bed; just then, his phone rang.

"Yo, what's good nigga?"

"Where the fuck you at man? You won't believe what the fuck is going on!"

"I'm umm...I'm..." Lando stuttered, noticing Chase was upset. His mind slipped to the St. Louis situation because he knew Cybo had been fucking up lately.

"Never mind that," Chase answered, realizing Lando was stuttering over his words. "Bruh...I think something may have happened to Kass."

Lando eyes widened. "What you mean, man? What's going on?" Lando questioned as he quickly jumped back into his clothes and sat on the bed to tie up his Timbs, phone cradled between his cheek and shoulder.

"Man I don't know, I'm not exactly sure. All I know is I'm parked by Kass' car and she ain't in it."

"What you mean you parked by Kass' car and she not in it? Why would she be in her car at six o'clock in the morning anyway?"

"Nah... listen bruh. I didn't go home last night. I'll run that shit down later but...on my way home this morning, right before the road to the house, I saw her car parked on side of the road. When I pulled over and looked inside, I saw her bags in there like she packed 'em to leave or some shit. Fuck! Maybe she was leaving because I stayed out all night–fuck, fuck, fuck!"

"Wait, wait...calm down bruh. So Kass probably was leaving you because you stayed out all night, but her car is on the side of the road empty and she's nowhere to be found?"

"Yeah man, yeah. Fuck man, what the fuck! I mean...I know I fucked up by staying out and shit, but why would her car just be here with bags and shit and she ain't even here?"

"Yo son...that shit sounds foul as fuck. I'm on my way now," Lando said.

"Hold up, wait a minute! Did I just hear you say something about Kassidy's car is parked somewhere but she's not in it? What the fuck?!" Mia asked as she jumped out of the bed.

"Yeah ma, something like that I guess. Fuck man! Man I hope that nigga Zo ain't got ahold of Kass or no shit like that. This can't be good yo."

Mia eyes widened, and her mouth dropped. "What? What the fuck is going on? Who the fuck is Zo and why would he want to take Kassidy?" Mia questioned.

"I don't know, I gotta go find out. I'll hit you up later," Lando said as he rushed out the bedroom.

"But wait..." Mia said as she followed Lando, but he kept walking and then went right out of the door.

"What the fuck is going on!" Mia said out loud as she threw her hands up. She ran to her room and got her phone, then dialed Kassidy. Kassidy's phone didn't ring; instead, it went straight to the voicemail.

What the fuck. No man, this shit can't be real. Kass can't be missing...right?

Chapter 25

Lando met Chase on the side of the road as he stood backed up against Kassidy's car with his hands inside of his pockets. Lando pulled to the side and parked behind Chase's truck. He jumped out and walked towards Chase. He reached his hand out, dapped him up, half-hugging him as they did a chest-to-chest bump. Lando then stood a few inches away from Chase, facing the car as Chase stood backed up against it.

"Chase bruh...this shit looks real foul if you ask me. I mean, why would Kass leave her car on the side of the road like this?"

"Yeah, the more I think about it, it just don't feel right. Something else is definitely going on, other than her leaving me because I ain't come home last night. I just checked my voicemail and Rick left me a shitload of messages about her taking off. He even said she pulled out on him."

"A pistol?" Lando asked as his eyes widened.

"Yeah dogg, a pistol. I got her one after that shit happened with that nigga Zo."

"About that...do you think...I mean, is it even possible that the nigga got a hold of Kass?"

"Fuck, anything is possible–ya feel me? At this point, I ain't ruling shit out. I mean, niggas coming at us all kinds of ways lately. They hit St. Louis, that bitch ass nigga came into my house, and now this. These niggas must got me fucked up, for real."

"Word. Did you try calling her?"

"Course I did. Went straight to voicemail."

Lando crossed his arms across his chest and placed one hand on his chin. "So how you wanna handle this shit, bruh?"

"First and foremost, I need to find out what happened to my baby. Man fuck, that bitch Meka asked me to have a drink with her ass last night, and that's why I wasn't fucking home."

"Meka, nigga what? You mean to tell me you was with that bitch last night?"

Chase inhaled and exhaled at Lando's remark. "Yeah man, unfortunately. Shit wasn't planned, just kind of happened. I was too fucked up to drive–so she says so anyway." Lando looked at Chase strangely as he continued to stand with his arms folded and chin resting in-between his thumb and pointing finger.

"Dogg, you never get that bent. I mean...you always on alert. And what you mean *so she says?* Like you don't remember or some shi–hold up, what's that underneath the car?" Lando asked as he noticed something black on the pavement.

Chase stepped forward and took a look. He then walked closer to the door and kneeled down. He reached his hand underneath and pulled out Kassidy's phone.

"What the fuck! And her phone is left behind? Nigga this shit ain't no motherfucking joke. Something definitely happened to my girl," Chase said as he noticed the battery and back of Kassidy's phone. He slid his hand underneath the car again, grabbing all parts of the phone. He then put the phone back together and pressed the power button. Chase stood up as he waited for Kassidy's phone to load. He looked at her call history to see who she called last, and then he looked at her messages to see who she last sent messages to or received any from.

"What the fuck is this?" Chase said out loud as he clicked on a message that came from Meka's number. Lando walked closer, and Chase pressed play on the video attachment. Lando and Chase witnessed firsthand his own dick sliding in and out of Meka's ass.

"Imma kill that bitch, I swear! That hoe set me up!" Chase said as he looked at Lando.

"That hoe down bad for that shit, son."

"Check it...you go see if you can find out where that nigga Zo at right now, just in case he had anything to do with Kass disappearing. Get them niggas ready because we need to make a

move, and I mean quick. In the meantime, I need to go break this bitch's neck."

"Aight man," Lando answered as he dapped Chase up before turning to leave. "Don't worry dog...we gon' find out exactly what happened and we will find Kass–I put that on everything."

Chase was so furious he couldn't even respond. Lando let his hand go, and Chase walked off and got into his truck. His tires were spinning and he hadn't even pulled off yet. Skid marks streaked the ground as Chase did a hundred miles down the road, heading to the interstate. What would normally be a thirty-minute drive only took him fifteen. He pulled up in front of Meka's condo and jogged to her front door. As Meka was getting ready for work, the loud noise of her door coming off the hinges startled her. She ran out of her bedroom and into her living room.

"What the fuck is going on!" she yelled as she noticed Chase had kicked down her door and entered her living room.

"Hoe, you know exactly what's going on!" Chase said as he charged toward Meka and grabbed her around her throat, leaving her legs dangling. "Bitch, you playing with me huh, you playing with me? You set me up, didn't you! Where is she? Your bitch ass sent a motherfucking video to Kassidy, where is she!"

Meka's eyes watered as she struggled to breathe. She fought to get Chase's hands from around her neck as his grip got tighter the more she tried to break free. Chase threw Meka into the wall, creating a hole the size of her body. Meka fell to the floor and coughed as she gasped for air to breathe.

"Cha...uh...Chas...plea..." she cried as she tried to call out Chase's name and beg him to stop.

Chase grabbed Meka up by her hair and put his gun to her head. "Bitch, you better start talking or I will blow your muhfuckin' brains out."

"Okay, okay," Meka cried as she noticed hate in Chase's eyes–a side of him she had never seen before, and she instantly

regretted that she let Zo drag her into the whole scheme to set him up.

"Bitch, I said where the fuck is she!" Chase yelled as he shifted a round into the chamber of his Glock.

"Zo, it was Zo...he made me do it. He has her."

Chase huffed and puffed, and his trigger finger was itching to cancel Meka right then and there, but he had bigger fish to fry. She told him Zo had Kassidy, and he knew he needed to get to Zo because he wasn't sure what he would do to her.

"Give me that motherfucking video camera."

Meka eased from the floor, barely moving because of the bodily harm Chase had inflicted on her. She walked to her bedroom as Chase followed behind her. She passed Chase the camera and he opened it up to find the memory card still inside.

"Is this the card?"

Meka shook her head yes, and she trembled with fear as tears fell from her eyes. The back of Chase's hand met her face, and she went sliding again across the floor.

"If anything happens to her, I will kill you," Chase affirmed as he walked out of Meka's room, then out of her apartment.

Chapter 26

Head stuffy and suffering from a serious case of cottonmouth, Kassidy slowly opened her eyes and took in her surroundings. *Oh no! Where am I? Wait, where's Chase!"* she panicked inwardly. Attempting to roll onto her side and sit up to get her bearings together. Her efforts were halted when she was forcibly snatched back by the wrist restraints she hadn't noticed before. Her mind flashed back to the night she'd been sleeping peacefully and awakened to a gun resting at her temple, after which she was tied to a chair and mocked by the man she now knew was Zo.

Although her first instinct was to scream, she bit her tongue and remained quiet, fighting to relax her respirations as she thought back on the last thing she remembered. *Shit, my phone!* her eyes widened in fear as she realized that wherever she was, she likely wouldn't be able to let Chase or anyone else know since she didn't have her phone. Just as she craned her neck to look at what was restraining her wrists, the door to the room opened. Yet again, she felt a bit of déjà vu as her eyes came to rest on the face of her uninvited visitor from a few months back–Zo.

"And so we meet again. I trust you've been resting well?" Zo smiled, almost as if he wasn't holding Kassidy against her will. Kassidy remained silent, but her chest heaved up and down in anger.

"Now I'll assume that you gave your little corner boy my message, but if I know that ego of his, he likely just brushed it off and figured I'd step off and let things smooth over–am I right?" Zo probed a still-silent Kassidy.

"It's okay, words aren't really necessary for what I have planned for us," Zo's lips curled in a menacing smile; that last statement got Kassidy's attention.

"Look, I don't know what issue you have with Chase, but I'm not a part of that…and I promise I won't tell anyone if you just let–"

"Well now, I know good girls like yourself don't usually kiss and tell, but it will be completely up to you whether you choose to air your dirty laundry or not," Zo taunted. Realizing the intent behind his statement, Kassidy's face finally registered the one emotion she'd been trying to suppress–panic. Reading the alarm in her eyes, Zo closed the distance between them and sat on the bed next to Kassidy.

"Relax preciosa…" he whispered as he leaned in closer to her neck, drawing in a long whiff of her scent. "Mmm… I smell fear when I'd much rather smell the scent of gratification on this beautiful flesh of yours, preciosa," Zo continued, tracing his index finger along Kassidy's jaw line. *Oh no…Kassidy* quietly panicked.

Kassidy forced her face into a stern scowl, but inside she felt something very different…very…unexpected…very…confusing–Zo was turning her the fuck on. He was dressed casually in an orange Balmain cashmere sweater and a pair of distressed biker jeans of the same brand. Despite the fact that most of his flesh was hidden from her view, Kassidy could easily see the ripple of muscles that screamed against the fabric of his sweater. His closely cropped curls were neatly edged up, and his sideburns were thinly trimmed to perfection as they extended into a closely sheared goatee. Kassidy fought to mask her low-key inspection of the six feet of Dominican deliciousness that hovered a little too close to her face for comfort.

"Preciosa…how long do you think it will be before you are begging to feel…good?" Kassidy met his question with another stoic stare, lips pressed tightly to suppress the slight moan that threatened to betray her tough exterior.

"Oh you will…you'll give it willingly," Zo smiled, tracing his finger down the side of her neck, across her collarbone, and down the delicate crevice between her breasts.

Shit…what the fuck? Why does this man…feel so good in my space, Kassidy silently probed herself. She was torn to say the least. This was the same man that invaded the safety and privacy of her

home, the same man that threatened *her man*, and the same man that had somehow taken her against her will. She knew she should be raging mad, but for some reason that she couldn't understand, she felt surprisingly at ease with Zo all up in her space–at ease and highly aroused.

Reading Kassidy's internal battle through her eyes, Zo continued his exploration. He alternated tracing the bottom of her breasts, occasionally steering off course to circle her nipples, which quickly grew into what he imagined were a chocolate-hued set of gumdrops.

"Now your eyes may be saying no… but I would bet that your popola is saying something to the contrary," Zo winked as his hand skated down Kassidy's abdomen, gently fingering the heart-shaped jewelry that adorned her navel.

Kassidy's body tensed as she anticipated where his hands would land next; she didn't have to wait long as Zo's hand gently tugged at the waistline of her floral Bebe joggers. Slipping two fingers behind the elastic, he journeyed a little farther down, now tracing the smoothness of her vagina courtesy of a thorough Brazilian wax. Shifting his gaze back up to her face, Zo saw that Kassidy's resistance was slowly faltering as evidenced by the fierce nibbling her teeth were giving her bottom lip. *Must…hold…back,* Kassidy's brain willed the rest of her body to resist.

Zo extended his index finger further south and down her landing strip before reaching his intended destination. Parting her lips gently, his finger slipped between the wetness of her folds. Tracing a path back north, Zo's fingertip came to rest on her love button, which seemed to throb under his touch. No longer able to feign disinterest, Kassidy's body succumbed to Zo's tantalizing seduction as a breathy moan slipped past her lips, which were now slippery courtesy of her tongue.

"It would seem that popola is in need…will you grant her what she needs, preciosa?" Zo locked eyes with Kassidy, sending his

lustful intentions in a brooding glare; Kassidy clamped her legs together even tighter, hoping to suppress the trickle that threatened to flow below. *Please stop,* Kassidy begged of her moist center, which was slowly growing into an urging inferno under Zo's caressing.

"Perhaps we should let popola speak for herself...shall we do that?" Kassidy squirmed underneath Zo's touch as yet another moan rose from her throat. Determined to make her give in, Zo headed south, now tracing the edge of Kassidy's opening; his efforts were met with an even louder moan that time. The tension in her thighs was gradually slipping away as her throbbing moisture willed her to succumb to what would no doubt be a fuck to remember.

"What's that? Ahh...popola is such a meek soul...perhaps we just need to have a one-on-one conversation...do you think she would like that?" Zo probed as he rose to his feet and walked around to the foot of the bed.

Leaning over and reaching for Kassidy's waistband, he tugged slightly to slide her joggers underneath the plumpness of her ass; his tugging was short-lived as Kassidy's hips raised the tiniest bit to aid his removal. Zo cast a lustful smile toward her face as he relished the success of his efforts to force a willing compliance out of Kassidy without the use of force. He released his grip on her waistband and shifted his attention to the ankles of her pants, tugging at each of the legs and letting them fall to the floor between his feet. Since Kassidy was pantiless, Zo was now granted an unobstructed view of what he knew was for sure a delicious and delectable dessert.

Zo planted both hands on either side of Kassidy's legs as he leaned in and over the bed. He locked eyes with her for a few seconds, almost as if they were engaged in a stare down with a very heated nonverbal conversation bouncing back and forth between them. Even in his silence, he had a commanding energy that forced submission, hence the reason he was chosen to lead the Valentino

family dynasty back home. Where most drug lords wore reputations for using ruthless acts of violence to get what they wanted, Zo was quite the opposite. Everything about his aura oozed *dominance*, and while men were always too macho to initially do things his way, they always conceded in the end. Women, on the other hand, were usually swept in the moment they became entranced by his aquamarine blue eyes, and from the looks of things, Kassidy would be no different.

"Please don't..." Kassidy began as Zo eased closer to her; his chest was now mere inches from the top of her plentiful thighs. He licked his lips before lowering his face meet her landing strip. Maintaining a distance of a few inches, he once again gazed up into Kassidy's eyes to send yet another silent command. As if on cue, Kassidy eased her legs apart, granting Zo's body a more intimate entry into her space.

"Please don't stop? That is what you meant, right?" Zo spoke, his gaze now trained on her lips. He slid a single finger deep into Kassidy's wetness before she had a chance to respond. Caught off guard, Kassidy sucked in a sharp inhale as her pussy began a gushy chorus around Zo's finger; her wetness tricked down his hand and onto the bed linen below, forming a small pool where her ass met the linen.

Zo drilled his finger deep into her wetness, adding another as he leaned forward and teased her pertly erect clit with his breath. Kassidy mumbled a mouthful of intelligible pleas as Zo finally graced her button with his tongue–just the tip though. Kassidy whimpered her desire as her wrists writhed against the restraints. Zo began a rapid flick of his tongue in chorus with the drilling of his fingers. He strummed her center as though he were plucking the strings of a Fender Stratocaster, her moans providing the perfect vocal harmony.

"Please…" Kassidy pleaded yet again, although she wasn't sure if she was begging for Zo to cease his efforts or drop his clothes and use his *real* tool to drill into her sugary walls.

"Please what…" Zo prodded. Kassidy may have been confused about the intent of her please, but Zo knew this dance all too well; it was the reason he regularly found himself swimming is a sea of wetness from several different source springs.

"Please what?" Zo probed further when Kassidy failed to indulge his previous inquiry. Reading the blaze of need in her eyes, Zo withdrew his hand and returned to his standing position. Sliding his shirt up over his head, he added it to the pile of Kassidy's pants. Kassidy's eyes bucked as they came to rest on the brick wall of muscle that her loins rightly told her rested beneath his shirt. Zo resumed his position and phalangeal assault of her vaginal walls. Tongue back in place, he went into overdrive as he worked feverishly to bring Kassidy to the cusp of release. When he felt the tension return to her thighs and pelvis, signaling her imminent explosion, he halted his tongue and withdrew his fingers. Kassidy snapped her head up and looked on with a look of horror.

"Please what?" Zo asked one last time, already knowing the response that would greet him.

"Please…fuck…me…" and with that, Zo's mouth curved into a smile of accomplishment. He once again returned to his feet, this time releasing the buttons of his jeans. As he slid the Balmain boxer briefs down, his dick sprang free, pointing straight ahead at his newest victory. He slid the remainder of his clothing to the floor and climbed onto the bed, his body hovering just inches above Kassidy's. Reaching down to grab his pole, he playfully tapped her clit with the tip, sending her into a mock hyperventilation. Her back bucked against the mattress as she spread her legs even farther apart to accommodate Zo's massive frame. Now pelvis to pelvis, Zo brought his lips just above Kassidy's mouth.

"Ask and ye shall receive," he whispered to her j
her eyes grew wide with surprise at the unexpected plung
dick deep into her sugar pool.

*Fuck...what the fuck am I doing?? But damn...this n
feels too gooooooood....*

'er 27

ust before
e of his
igga

⌣hase by kidnapping his precious
court. As Chase had said, *Zo wanted*
ᴎ just the way to go about getting it.
ᴐ had his way with Chase's pride and joy,
ᴧe right places as her body failed her by
s tantalizing seduction and his almost edible
ɟ felt torn and conflicted as her mind played tricks
ᴣ her crammed with guilt that she actually enjoyed
ᴠith a man who would go as far as kidnapping her. The
ᴌassidy was still madly in love with Chase didn't help her
. struggle either.

Zo returned Kassidy to her home; safe, sound, and thoughtful
. all the dirty little deeds that he'd bestowed to her. Although Zo
abducted Kassidy, he treated her like a princess and in a strange way,
Kassidy knew that he would not harm her–other than making her
body desire him.

After being at her own home and collecting her thoughts,
Kassidy finally called Chase from her home phone to let him know
that she had been returned. Chase raced over to her place and was
thrilled to learn that Zo didn't take something away from him that
meant the world to him; the love of his life. Little did Chase know,
Zo had other plans for Kassidy and in due time, he would soon learn
of them. Chase called his dogs off for the meantime and decided to
come up with a more thorough and strategic plan to go up against
Zo, who was obviously out to destroy him and everything that he
loved.

Kassidy was still upset to find out that the man she loved
betrayed her with the woman he said meant nothing to him. She
couldn't understand how Chase could recklessly sacrifice her heart
and fuck Meka like they were aiming for an adult entertainment
Oscar. Chase tried his damndest to plead his case, and he

remembered he made Meka give him the memory card. He then explained to Kassidy that meeting up with Meka wasn't planned, and that she had been replaced by another realtor he acquired who was helping him find a new house. Kassidy's abduction was the final straw, and Chase knew he had to relocate ASAP.

Chase showed Kassidy the parts in the video where he appeared to be more than drunk and he told Kassidy he believed Meka drugged him, and how he got her to confess everything, which was how he found out that Zo had taken her. After painfully watching her man fuck another woman, Kassidy realized there was more to the story than the clip that Meka sent to her, and she also despised Zo for going that far to get to Chase, but she was having a struggle convincing her body of that.

A month had passed, and Kassidy was back at Chase's place. They were trying to move forward after realizing they both were a part of Zo and Meka's fuckery to build a wedge of distrust between the two of them.

"What time will you be back bae?" Kassidy pouted, genuinely disappointed that Chase had to step out to handle some business yet again.

"It won't be long ma, promise," Chase smiled, pulling her into a caring embrace as he rained a flurry of kisses up and down her cheeks.

"Uh huh, that's why her ass all spoiled and shit now," Mia jokingly rolled her eyes at the couple.

Since Kassidy's abduction, Chase was more overprotective than ever, barely letting her leave his sight to use the restroom. He'd asked Lando to hit Mia up and have her come over to keep Kassidy company since they had some business to tend to. Chase didn't want Kassidy alone and truthfully, Kassidy didn't want to be alone with her thoughts and intrusive daydreams. Chase had hired an extra security team just to cover his house, and upgraded the surveillance

and security systems; all things considered, Kassidy was probably better protected now as the bank vault in the basement at Fort Knox.

"Shut up heifer, you just mad cuz you ain't got a boo–yet," Kassidy teased as she cast a knowing glance at Lando. Things between he and Mia had really been heating up, despite the fact that he was very much still a married man, but he was being smart about his moves so far, keeping their little fling under wraps for the most part. Chase and Kassidy were really the only ones that knew about them, and Lando intended to keep it that way.

"Aight ma, we gotta bounce, I'll call you though, and no–"

"I know, I know…" Kassidy interrupted, "NO leaving the house for any reason," she rehearsed what had become Chase's mantra anytime he stepped out nowadays. Chase knew he was being overprotective, but aside from sending Kassidy away to an undisclosed location, it was the only way he knew to try to keep her out of Zo's reach.

"Okay," Kassidy frowned just as Chase exited, closed the door behind him. Just as Kassidy turned to rejoin Mia in the kitchen, a wave of dizziness rushed over her body. Since her bizarre tryst with Zo, she'd been having anxiety attacks on and off, especially when either she or Chase left the house. She wouldn't even ride in her old car anymore after being kidnapped, so Chase had replaced it with the Tesla Model X.

"You okay girl?" Mia jumped up and crossed the floor, grabbing onto Kassidy's shoulders. "I told you to chill with all that damn coffee; you gonna fuck around and OD on caffeine up in here," Mia scolded. She'd witnessed a few of Kassidy's dizzy spells, one of which actually caused her to pass out. They hadn't told Chase though, hoping to avoid kicking his exaggerated overprotection to an even higher level.

"Uhh yeah, I'm good. Maybe you're right, all that coffee is clogging my system up and shit. I just need some water. I'm probably dehydrated or something," Kassidy reasoned as she

resumed her seat on the barstool, crossing her legs Indian-style. "Thanks," she beamed at Mia as she reached out to grab the bottle of Fiji, turning it up and chugging half the bottle in just a few gulps.

"Witcho thirsty ass," Mia laughed before resuming her spot on the stool next to Kassidy. "You know what your problem is?" Mia dropped her voice to barely above a whisper, trying to keep the home monitoring system from hearing what she said. "You still thinking 'bout that nigga Zo and shit. Hell, I don't blame you. If he a G like you said he was then shit, I'd still be thinking 'bout that D too," Mia whispered before erupting into a fit of laughter.

"Shut the hell up Mia! Ain't nobody thinking about him," Kassidy shushed her friend. "I just can't help but be worried about Chase whenever he leaves," her mood shifted as her thoughts returned to the apple of her eye.

"Girl, you act like that nigga ain't the king of Staten Island and shit. That nigga security detail is like the secret service. He gon' be just fine," Mia smacked her lips before returning to her magazine article and a bowl of grapes. She popped a few grapes in her mouth before continuing. "I still think you should tell him…if he finds out later, it's gonna make it look like something it wasn't," Mia advised, never taking her eyes off the article on the *Top 10 Aphrodisiac Foods That Feed Your Sex Drive*. Mia's words resonated with Kassidy for the next few minutes. Mia was right about Zo still being on her mind, but she'd never admit it. She knew she fucked up by not letting Chase know something happened when she first got back home, but she just didn't know how to go about telling him now without coming off like she was hiding something else from him.

***

"Aight, one," Lando ended his phone call before turning to Chase, who drove them up NY 440 toward the warehouse. "Them niggas had eyes on him all day, he's headed up that way now, so we'll be posted up waiting when that fool fall through," Lando relayed the info he'd just received from his caller.

"And you sure that bird ain't on some setup shit?" Chase questioned again; he didn't care how good her pussy was to Lando, she was still a thirsty ass chick in his eyes.

"Nigga, Mia cool. She might have a bad rap for shit she done in the past, but baby girl ain't on that *get money* shit no more."

"Uh huh, so if you was a broke nigga workin' the drive-thru she'd still rock wit you, right?" Chase countered with a sly grin as they pulled up behind their warehouse. Chase made sure to park out front in plain view so the nigga DeMarco would know they were there and fall right into the trap they had set for him.

"Whatever nigga, let's just get this shit over with and lay this nigga down so I can get back and slide up in some pussy," Lando called over his shoulder as they exited Chase's truck.

Inside, they made sure everyone was in place before disappearing down the hall to Chase's office. Lando brought Chase up to speed on how stuff was going out in St. Louis until one of their soldiers alerted them to DeMarco's arrival.

"Showtime my nigga," Lando smiled.

"Just like old times," Chase nodded.

The two of them made their way back down the hall to the room that connected to the dock area. There were two tractor-trailers backed in, and a handful of workers that ran back and forth unloading their latest shipment. Just as expected, they were joined by an uninvited guest.

"Y'all niggas ready to die today?" DeMarco boasted, shooting knowing glances at his bootleg clique of corner boys as they trained their weapons on Chase and Lando. Hearing the foreign voice boom throughout the room, two of Chase's workers scrambled to run to his aid, but Chase quickly shot them a look from the corner of his eye letting them know to stand down and remain hidden.

"You offering or making a request?" Chase smiled, crossing his arms across his chest. Lando stood to his left, hand lightly resting on the Glock that he had tucked into the back waistband of his jeans.

"Lemme guess…you thought you was gonna run up in here and hit my shit, right? Like I'm new to this shit, huh? See, lettin' a clown ass nigga catch you slippin' is a move yo' bitch ass might make, but if you had paid attention all this time you mighta learned something," Chase scolded just as DeMarco and his boys heard the distinct sound of metal on metal from behind. Frozen in place, DeMarco tried to get a glimpse of what was going on out of the corner of his eye while he kept his gun aimed at Chase.

"Nigga, you been hearin' my name in these streets since fuckin' middle school and this the best you can do? Run up in my shit with yo' lil fraud ass crew from the fuckin' playground?" Chase taunted. DeMarco was clearly nervous and second-guessing his attempt to come up at Chase's expense, as evidenced by the beads of sweat that now dotted his forehead.

"What was your question again? Are we ready to die today?" Chase frowned, feigning confusion. "Nah, but you are," Chase quipped before turning to walk away. Before he could take more than three steps, DeMarco and his crew were each met with a round to the back the head. The sprinkle of brain matter marked the cement floor where Chase and Lando had just departed from. Lando glanced over his shoulder at one of the workers that lay and wait for further direction.

"Get the crew out here to clean this shit up, then finish packin' that shit in the vault," Lando ordered.

Chapter 28

The situation with DeMarco handled and the shipment tucked away safely, Lando and Chase had made it back to the house and went their separate ways. Lando was now at Mia's spot to bust one last nut before he headed home to his wife.

"Ay ma, so check it, Chase gotta dip outta town for a bit so Imma hold shit down at the crib; you know he ain't bout to have Kass bein' alone and shit. You gon' come keep me company?" Lando asked.

"I don't know about all that; how is Chase gonna feel about that? You know that nigga be throwin' shade and shit," Mia rolled her eyes, even though she was excited at the thought of having Lando all to herself for more than a few hours at a time.

"Chill ma, you ain't gotta worry 'bout all that; so you comin' or nah?"

"How your wife gonna feel about you being gone and shit?" Mia bit her lip as soon as she'd finished, hoping her comment wouldn't kill the mood and set Lando off.

"Ay girl, what I tell you about that? When I'm wit you, I'm wit you. Ain't no need for you to even be bringing that shit up," Lando hissed, referring to his marriage.

"Okay, okay…I'm sorry…I was just sayin'…never mind…but yeah, you know Imma be there," Mia smiled as she eased down onto his lap, hoping to redirect his energy to more important things.

"Aight then–hop on this dick so I can roll out then," Lando smacked Mia's ass as she moved her thong to the side and slid down onto his dick as Future's lyrics danced through the air.

Baby let's go and have rich sex
Make a little love, have rich sex
Baby let's go and have rich sex

Baby girl, let's have some rich sex

Five minutes later, Mia was overflowing with excitement at the thought of playing house with Lando. Just the thought of finally being able to fuck him all night and wake up in his arms pushed her over the top, and she rained her orgasm down all over Lando's lap.

"Ahhhh shiiiiiiit ma!" Lando boomed shortly after, sending a million soldiers marching all up and through Mia's walls of temptation.

This girl gon' fuck around and have me caught up; pussy is A-fuckin' one.

***

Once Lando left, Mia hopped in the shower and settled in to thumb through the thick envelope that was delivered via FedEx earlier that day. One of the reasons Mia and Kassidy had become quick friends was because of their mutual dislike of their parents' ways. For Mia, it was her mother who gave her indigestion. She loved her to death, but she just couldn't deal with her lies and secrets.

One of the biggest lies she'd ever pulled off was allowing Mia to grow up thinking that her stepfather was her birth father. It wasn't until Mia was applying for a passport her senior year that she discovered the truth, courtesy of her birth certificate. Mia found it odd that the Father field read *Unknown*, especially since her parents were married the same year that she was born. Confronting her mother in a rage, Mia learned that her mother was already pregnant by another man when she married Mia's stepfather, who was as good a father as any kid could hope for, but the fact still remained that he wasn't *her* father.

When Mia pressed her mother as to the identity of her biological father, as was her usual practice when she was hiding something, her mother had shut down and refused to speak about the situation. This sent them into a silent standoff as neither spoke to the

other, which was customary in their dysfunctional mother-daughter relationship.

Refusing to settle for her mother's indifference in this situation, Mia hired an investigator to do some digging and help her find out the identity of her real father. The envelope had been delivered to Mia's neighbor's house earlier that day, and since Lando had called saying he was on the way as she was walking through the door, Mia hadn't had a chance to peruse the content like she wanted—that and she was too busy bouncing up and down Lando's dick like she was at a rodeo.

Hands shaking and heart racing a mile a minute, Mia braced herself for what the contents would reveal. On the top of the stack were several photos, presumably taken while the man was in his late teens to early twenties. Her mother was pictured in one of the photos, giving Mia reassurance that the information was indeed on the right track.

Placing the photos to the side, she turned her attention to several papers, some of which appeared tattered and worn with time. Her eyes eagerly digested the contents, seeking that one vital piece of information that would tie it all together. As she reached the final page of the stack, her eyes zoomed in on what she was looking for. Thinking her eyes were playing tricks on her, she read over the block of text over and over, shocked into utter silence. *It can't be...there's no fucking way...how the...did he know? Has he known all this time? What the hell?* Mia's mind was racing a mile a minute as she jumped up, slid into a pair of PINK joggers and a racerback tank, and slipped her feet into her Uggs. Grabbing her keys from the kitchen counter, she snatched her phone and MK clutch up as she dashed out the door to her car.

This bitch got some serious fuckin' explaining to do!

Chapter 29

"Mmmm, I got sumthin' to fill ya mouth, gurl," Chase smiled.

"You promise, cause all I'm hearin' is talk… we'll see what you workin' with when you touch down. When are you comin' back anyway, babe?" Kassidy cooed.

"Soon ma," Chase began, but paused as he turned onto the unpaved trail leading up to the safe house. "Ay ma, lemme hit you back in a lil' bit," Chase hesitated.

"Okay bae, love you–" Kassidy began before realizing that Chase had abruptly disconnected the call. Just then, she felt yet another wave of dizziness wash over her as an uneasy feeling took up residence in the pit of her stomach. Chase never ended calls without telling Kassidy he loved her.

Luckily for her, she was already stretched across the bed, so there was no threat of her passing out on the floor. Kassidy lay there a few more minutes waiting for the room to stop spinning before she tried to sit up. Thankfully, she had a doctor's appointment that afternoon to speak with the doctor about her anxiety and dizziness. Her mother, Maria, had urged her to make an appointment out of concern for an early onset of hypertension. Maria had the same set of symptoms when she was around Kassidy's age, and it had been a struggle ever since to manage the condition, especially since it required her to limit her intake of all the foods she loved, and those that brought her comfort. Living with Kameron Kingston was anything but easy; the stress of that alone was enough to send her into a stroke, so Maria was gravely concerned with Kassidy's symptoms.

Since Chase had her on a leash whenever he wasn't around, he'd assigned Rick to be her personal bodyguard, so he'd drive her to her appointment that day.

"Look, before you even say anything, I do NOT need you coming in with me. Bad enough I feel like I got LoJack installed on my ass and shit," Kassidy snapped.

"Girl I don't care what you want, my orders are not to take my eyes off you, so you might as well be easy over there," Rick emphasized. Since he spent so much time around Kassidy, their rapport had evolved into a playful one, almost like a sibling rivalry–that was the only reason Kassidy tolerated his slick mouth. She sharply exhaled before responding.

"Look, can you at least wait in the hall? I don't need you all up in the waiting room and shit. You know you look like a big ass bear, and ain't nobody tryin' to have you posted up in the corner lookin' all scary and shit," Kassidy half-joked.

"I got your bear. Come on 'fore you be late."

Kassidy hadn't even been checked in and seated for five minutes before she was called to the back.

"Kassidy Kingston," the medical assistant called as she stepped into the waiting room. After giving blood and urine samples, Kassidy was placed in an examination room. She took a seat in one of the chairs adjacent to the simplified workstation that sat next to the counter and sink area.

"Good afternoon Ms. Kingston," the doctor entered a short time later.

"Hi Doctor Sipley," Kassidy smiled.

"So what brings you here today?" the doctor probed before Kassidy gave her an abbreviated summary of the issues and symptoms she'd been having over the past few months.

"I see," the doctor began. "And you say that you haven't been experiencing any other notable symptoms of concern?"

"No ma'am," Kassidy confirmed; the doctor paused before continuing.

"Well Ms. Kingston, although the dizziness and fainting are some of the less common symptoms of your condition. Congratulations, you are going to be a mommy!" Dr. Sipley beamed. "I believe that they are not of significant concern at the moment. I do, however, want to…" the doctor continued, but Kassidy's mind had zoned off upon mention that she was pregnant. Suddenly, Mia's words twirled through her head as she began to feel dizzy under the weight of the bomb Dr. Sipley had just dropped. *"I still think you should tell him…if he finds out later, it's gonna make it look like something it wasn't."*

Shit!

***

Ending the call, Chase stopped his truck a few feet short of the fence that hugged the property line, just beyond the eyeshot of the house. Sliding out of the driver seat, he softly eased the door shut, then took long, deliberate steps toward the house, tiptoeing across the gravel. *Something's off, shit ain't right,* he thought to himself as his feet came to rest at the trunk base of a Dominican Magnolia tree, which was in full bloom. Stilling his respirations, he slipped into his zone, shutting out all stimuli and clearing his head to assess just what the fuck had caused the eerie silence.

Drawing a deep breath in through his nostrils, Chase's sinuses were greeted by a pungent odor that he was all too familiar with-fresh gunpowder. *Fuck,* he silently cursed, a sense of alarm settling deep in his gut as he dreaded the scene that likely awaited him inside. *Perfect hideout in plain sight my ass.* Retrieving his phone from his pocket, he pressed his right thumbprint onto the home button, unlocking the device. Swiping right twice, he opened the iCam app and disabled the cameras that surveilled the home's exterior before returning the phone to his pocket.

Crossing the yard and hugging the right exterior wall of the home, Chase crept just under the first window, coming to rest underneath the second and only window that would afford him a 360

view of most of the first floor. Retrieving a small square of plastic from his pocket, he flipped it over, extended it a few inches from his face, and angled the mirrored back to face the window. Rotating the mirror from left to right a few times, he took in the view. *No bodies...the fuck is them niggas at?*

Chase side-stepped the remainder of the wall and arrived at the back door. Glock 40 drawn, he glanced around the backyard, hurdled the trip wire, and quickly ascended the stairs to step onto the oak floor just beyond the threshold. Body hugging the staircase, Chase eased toward the front entry of the home, pausing as he cleared one room after another. As he approached the third room to his left, he froze mid-step when he heard a faint rustling. Just as he craned his neck to hone in on the sound, the door came crashing open.

BLAH! BLAH! BLAH!

Chase dove away from the door just as a round zipped past his left temple; his right shoulder met the rigid floor with a thud as he returned fire, both set of rounds now mixed in a drafty joust.

"Ahh fuck!" Chase hissed as a bullet ricocheted off the door frame and pierced his left forearm. He slid across the floor, briefly retreating into the alcove provided by the previous doorway. Just as his back came to rest on the door, he heard a flurry of footsteps approach him. Wasting no time, he leaned forward, took aim outside the doorway, and started to empty his clip.

"Shit! Get back! Get back!" He heard the nigga throw a panicked warning to someone else, but it was too late. Chase looked on as the bodies of both niggas hit the floor—one face up, eyes glazed over in distress, and the other stretched out on his stomach, a mess of curls obscuring his forehead.

"Ugh...fuck...ahh..." curly top groaned, a stream of blood flowing onto the floor from his mouth.

Chase replaced his spent clip, briefly applied pressure to his wound, then rose to his feet and took a few short steps, stopping just short of the curly top's head.

"Turn over, nigga," Chase ordered, nudging the man's shoulder with his foot.

"Fuck you!" the man spat in return; Chase chuckled as he locked eyes with him, sending a sharp kick to the man's stomach. Now doubled over in pain, the man obliged Chase's request.

"Coño!" the man moaned.

"You joinin' ya homie ova there? Or you gon' tell me how the fuck you found my spot?" Chase quizzed.

"Maldito hijo de la porra, veta pa la porra!" curly top willed Chase to take a trip to hell.

"You first," Chase smiled just before he sent two rounds into the man, one to the dome, one to the chest.

Both men DOA, Chase stepped over their bodies and made his way to the foot of the stairs, careful to clear the area around him and watch his back. He made a deliberate ascension of the stairs, pausing once he was able to peer over the landing onto the second floor. The eerie calm that hung in the air, and that fact that no one had come to his aid, let Chase know that the small team he'd brought down to the DR with him was probably dead. Never one to back down from a fight, Chase had to keep pressing forward and make sure no one left that house alive—except for himself.

There were four doors, not including the bathroom that he'd have to clear alone and with no backup—not an ideal situation, but Chase had been in far worse predicaments. Since the two doors in front of him were open and granted a full view of the rooms, which had no closets, he presumed they posed the least threat. Instead, he turned his attention to the door on his left, which was slightly ajar. Retrieving his pocket mirror again, he positioned it to take in as much of the view beyond the door as he could. Just as Chase was zooming his view in on what appeared to be an object just behind the

door, that same door came crashing open, making way for the flurry of gunfire that erupted. Chase retreated a few feet and slammed his back against the wall, gun aimed at the top of the stairs.

When the gunfire stopped, he climbed a few more stairs and stopped two stairs short of the landing. The door was now fully ajar, and Chase wasted no time taking those last few stairs and throwing his body into the room and against the wall. Peering around the corner, he was met with another wave of gunfire. Chase dropped to the floor and crawled into one of the two rooms that he'd dismissed earlier. He flung the door shut, but not before the shooter kicked the door back open and made his entry.

"That Rambo shit might work in your *kingdom* in Staten Island, but this is MY shit! I run this country!"

"Then stay the fuck in YOUR country and stay the fuck outta mine, nigga!" Chase boomed, his finger gently squeezing the trigger.

"I'll give Ms. Kassidy *preciosa* your love," Zo taunted as he too squeezed the trigger of his own gun. Their eyes locked in an intense standoff, which ended in a split second when a shot rang out, followed by another.

"Ahhhhh shit!" one of the men yelled just before everything faded to black.

TO BE CONTINUED....

***** Thank You For Reading *****

Thank you so much for reading our novel!
Please don't forget to drop a review on Amazon–it will be greatly appreciated, and we would love to hear what you thought about this novel!

~

Don't forget to check out my other works as well:

I Should've Cheated (pen name TJ Rose)
Love, Betrayal, & Dirty Money (pen name TJ Rose)

~

Feel free to connect with me at:
Author website: www.authortjrose.com
Email: info@authortjrose.com
Twitter: @tjrose_author
Instagram: @tjrose_author

Facebook Page: Author Tysha Jordyn:
https://www.facebook.com/tysha.jordyn

Stop by & check out my blog, Tysha's Tea, at:
http://www.authortjrose.com/blog-1/

Don't miss your chance to snag exclusive sneak peaks of upcoming books and monthly giveaways (no purchase necessary!)
Subscribe at http://www.authortjrose.com/newsletter/

You can also connect with MyKisha Mac via her Social Networks.

Facebook: https://www.facebook.com/MyKisha.mac
Facebook: https://www.facebook.com/TheMyKishaMacExperience

Please feel free to like TMME page and get info of all up and coming releases and event dates.

Follow On Twitter: @lovejones007

Blog: https://MyKishamac4books.wordpress.com/

Email: mykishamac@gmail.com

All Eyes On Us Contest

To celebrate the release of Tysha Jordyn and MyKisha Mac's first collaboration, your purchase has made you eligible to enter a drawing to win an Amazon Kindle E-reader! Entry requirements are as follows:

- Subscribe to the Tysha Jordyn (TJ Rose) newsletter at http://www.authortjrose.com/newsletter/
- Send an email to info@authortjrose.com that contains the following information:
  - Be sure to include **AEOU-CONTEST** in the subject line.
  - Include a screenshot or email confirmation of your purchase of this title
  - Include screenshot of your review of this title posted on Amazon
  - Include a sentence that reads, "Everyone wants happiness, no one wants pain, but you can't have a rainbow without a little rain."

Each entry received will be entered into the drawing. Contest will close at 11:59PM EST on the 21st day following the original release date. The winner will notified via email; winner will also be announced across social media on Facebook, Instagram, and Twitter. Thanks so much for your support-stay tuned for more great releases from Tysha Jordyn and MyKisha Mac!

Text ROYALTY to 42828 to keep up with our new releases!

Looking for a publishing home?

Royalty Publishing House, Where the Royals reside, is accepting submissions for writers in the urban fiction genre. If you're interested, submit the first 3-4 chapters with your synopsis to submissions@royaltypublishinghouse.com. Check out our website for more information: www.royaltypublishinghouse.com.

Be sure to <u>LIKE</u> our Royalty Publishing House
page on Facebook